THESE STREETS AIN'T FOR EVERYBODY

THESE STREETS AIN'T FOR EVERYBODY

T.M JEFFERSON

Under the shimmer of stadium floodlights, the smell of chlorine filled the air, and excited chatter and anticipation buzzed around the Olympic-sized pool. It was a typical crisp fall evening at Lincoln High, a school renowned for its fierce rivalry in the realm of sports. The bleachers were a sea of school colors, where each cheer held a fragment of adolescent pride.

In the crowd, Justice Carter sat on a cold aluminum bench, her eyes glued to the cerulean expanse that held the heart of her family's hopes. Beside her, her father, Blake, leaned forward, his knuckles turning white as he clutched the edge of his seat. His dedication to his children was unshakeable, even in the face of life's toughest challenges.

Justice's eyes remained on the water, where her younger brother, Jamal, stood on the edge of the pool like a sleek predator, muscles taut and glistening with water droplets. A freshman in high school, Jamal was not just an athlete; he was the star of the school's swim team.

His swimming goggles rested on his forehead, revealing a determination that matched the fire in his family's eyes.

"Go, Jamal!" Justice's voice rose above the crowd as she cheered on her brother. Her eyes shone with pride, mirroring the intensity of her father's love for his children.

Blake, with his firm hands, squeezed Justice's shoulder. "He's got this, baby girl," he whispered, and his eyes sparkled with a warmth that had carried them through life's darkest moments.

The sound of the starting buzzer pierced the air, and Jamal shot through the water like a torpedo, sleek and powerful. Every stroke showcased the hours of dedication he had poured into his passion, a reflection of his father's support.

Blake and Justice exchanged a glance, sharing the silent acknowledgment of the love that bound their family. In the heart of the stadium, a connection that transcended the competition united them.

As the crowd roared and cheered, the Carters watched, knowing that in the water, Jamal was not just a young swimmer racing to victory, but he was their strength, their dreams, and the legacy of a family marked by love that went above and beyond.

Jamal Carter wasn't just a face in the crowded hallways of Lincoln High School; he was the poster boy of academic excellence, a student whose straight-A record spoke volumes about his ambition and intellect. From the classrooms to the quiet corners of the library, Jamal's achievements set him apart, paving the way for a future that transcended the boundaries of his suburban enclave.

Within the halls of Lincoln High, Jamal's thirst for knowledge and academic success became the stuff of legend. Teachers lauded his inquisitive mind, his dedication to learning clear in every crafted assignment and thought-provoking question. Jamal's classmates marveled at his ability to navigate the complex landscape of subjects, turning each class into an arena for intellectual exploration.

As a straight-A student, Jamal's name became synonymous with excellence. Whether it was acing exams, taking part in academic competitions, or contributing to extracurricular activities, he emerged as a standout figure within the scholastic tapestry of Lincoln High School. His achievements were not just personal triumphs, but a source of pride for the entire school community.

Amid the pages of textbooks and classroom discussions, Jamal's ambitions blossomed. He envisioned a future where his academic prowess would open doors to prestigious universities, setting the stage for a career that would transcend the boundaries of Bayside. College admissions, scholarships, and the prospect of a life beyond the streets became the driving force behind Jamal's pursuit of knowledge.

The locker room door swung open, and Jamal emerged, his triumphant energy filling the corridor. He was a towering figure, holding a six-foot trophy like a cherished heirloom, the golden medal around his neck shining in the artificial light. The media surged towards him, microphones thrust in his direction, capturing his youthful face flushed with the exhilaration of victory.

He gave the reporters a brief interview, his voice confident and humble, sharing the credit with his teammates and his dedication to the sport. As the cameras flashed and questions rained down, his eyes searched the crowd. Then, amid the chaotic scene, he spotted them.

Justice and Blake stood together, their smiles radiating pride as they locked eyes with their victorious champion. Justice couldn't contain her joy, her wide grin brimming. Blake's eyes glistened with pride and unspoken words of encouragement for his son.

Jamal's path through the media throng led him to his family. With the trophy in one hand and the gold medal hanging around his neck, he wrapped his arms around Justice and Blake in a triumphant hug.

Justice's enthusiasm spilled over. "You did it, Jamal! We knew you could!"

Blake echoed his daughter's sentiments. "Your mother would be so proud of you, son. She's watching over you tonight."

They shared a reflective moment during the celebration, their hearts heavy without the woman, who had been a loving wife and mother. But they also knew that her spirit lived on in the love and resilience that bound their family together.

After their moment, Jamal suggested a restaurant to celebrate his victory, and they agreed without hesitation. In the warm embrace of family, they left the arena, leaving behind the media and the competition. United, they would celebrate this triumph and remember the woman who would have been the loudest supporter that evening.

In the heart of their Queens, New York neighborhood, Blake Carter anchored the Carter family's life. He was the embodiment of the community spirit. His barbershop, Fresh Cutz, was an institution that had stood for over a decade. The shop's worn leather chairs and buzzing clippers were comforting fixtures for the locals.

It was a bright Saturday morning, and the bell above the barbershop door chimed as a young boy with a tapered fade darted in for a high-five from Blake, his hair already neat and trim from the barbershop's trademark service.

Blake's commitment to his community extended beyond just haircuts; every holiday eve, he threw open the barbershop's doors and offered free haircuts to the local youth. It was an act of kindness that eased the financial burden on parents and brought smiles to the faces of youngsters who stepped out of his shop looking sharp and confident.

Justice, fresh out of high school and contemplating her future, was there to witness her father's generosity in action. She had dreams and ambitions, and college was one of those possibilities. Blake, supportive as ever, wanted to see her soar, but understood the importance of letting her make her own choices.

Jamal, engrossed his books and schoolwork, focused on a mission. The promise he had made to his late mother resonated in every assignment he tackled and every test he aced. She had wished for him to graduate high school and find success, and Jamal was determined to honor her memory.

Amidst the lively narrative of their lives, there was another constant — Blake's athletic dedication. He was a man who, four days a week, laced up his running shoes and hit the streets, conquering three to five miles with each stride. His love for sports and staying fit was not only for his own well-being but a lesson he wanted to instill in his children, showing them the value of maintaining a healthy body and a powerful spirit.

The modest townhouse in Bay-side Queens, where the

Carters called home, was a haven within the chaotic city. It was a place where family bonds ran deep, where dreams and aspirations were shared at the dinner table, and where the love that held them together was as tangible as the air they breathed.

Blake Carter, with his warm smile, was the family's backbone, the force that kept them united. As they weathered life's storms, the Carters knew that their unity would carry them through whatever challenges lay ahead.

Blake Carter's rhythmic footfalls along the East River created a sense of distance from the city's fast pace, implying a well-controlled life. The skyline, cast in hues of dawn, provided a picturesque backdrop to his daily run. He took care of his family's security and well-being, thrived in his barbershop, and committed himself to staying in peak physical condition.

But then, without warning, a dizziness swirled around him. It was as if the ground had shifted beneath him, and the expanse of the river became a disorienting blur.

Gasping for breath, he stumbled to a halt, trying to steady himself. His vision blurred. Seated on a bench, his pulse raced and the world wobbled. The East River, so serene a moment ago, now appeared as a turbulent force, mirroring the storm inside his body.

Beside him, an older Black man with a full white beard and a bald head observed his ordeal with knowing eyes. His voice was soothing amid Blake's disarray. "You're working too hard, young man," the stranger said. "Sometimes, life needs us to slow down."

Blake nodded, grateful for the advice, but as soon as the

dizziness subsided, he pushed himself to his feet and continued his run. The city's rhythm called to him, and he couldn't ignore it, not when providing for his family was his solemn duty.

Time passed, and the older gentleman's advice stayed with Blake. But slowing down wasn't an option for him; too much depended on his dedication.

The moment of reckoning arrived while at his barbershop, Fresh Cutz. The familiar scent of hair products filled the air, along with the buzz of clippers and the chorus of conversations. Blake was in his element, trimming a young man's hair as if he were sculpting a work of art.

But then it happened again. That staggering dizziness returned, intensified, and like a mighty wave crashing into him, it knocked him off balance. His vision blurred, the room spun, and the floor rushed up to meet him.

He crumpled to the ground, unconscious, surrounded by the familiar faces of his coworkers. Panic filled the air as they called for an ambulance, their voices trembling with concern.

In the silence of unconsciousness, Blake was oblivious to the surrounding commotion. His life, once controlled, now hung on the edge of uncertainty. The hospital awaited him. Unaware, his family was about to enter a world of fear, emotions, and unanswered questions.

The fluorescent lights buzzed overhead. As Justice clutched her phone, the call from the hospital had shattered her world. She knew she had to be strong, for her father, for Jamal. Panic clawed at her throat as she rushed to pick up her younger brother from school. The somber drive to the hospital was filled with a silence, punctuated only by Jamal's anxious glances at his sister.

Entering the room, they were greeted by the faces of

medical professionals, each stare heavy with unspoken truths. Their father lay in a hospital bed, a frail shadow of the man they had always known. Tubes and wires snaked across his body, and the machines beside him monitored life's fragile threads.

Justice whispered soothing words to Jamal, her arm wrapped around his shoulders. She took a deep breath, her eyes locking with her brothers, as if they were drawing strength from each other. They couldn't let their emotions consume them now; their father needed them more than ever.

As they approached the bed, the tears they had been holding back flowed. Justice's voice trembled as she whispered, "Dad, it's us. We're here."

Jamal, strong and focused, couldn't contain his grief, and tears rained down his face as he clutched their father's frail hand.

Blake's eyes fluttered open, and he managed a weak, but loving, smile, his hand trembling as he reached out to touch Jamal's face. He struggled to form the words, but they were filled with love and pride. "My... my champions," he said.

Emotions swelled, releasing sorrow, fear, and love. The raw vulnerability they had tried to conceal broke free, and they wept together, sharing the weight of the crushing news. A moment where words were needless.

Their world had changed, and the future seemed stormy with uncertainty. But for now, in this painful moment, the family clung to each other, their hearts knit together by the shared burden of their father's fate.

The passage of time witnessed a heart-wrenching transformation in Blake's condition. The cancerous tumor, a merciless intruder in his once-vibrant life, continued its assault on his body. Weeks passed, and the once strong man became a mere shadow of his former self.

Blake's skin had turned a sickly shade of dark gray, rough and blotchy, like a canvas marred by the harshest brushstrokes of suffering. His hair, once thick and black, was a distant memory, replaced by the barren expanse of his scalp. The weight loss had been dramatic, reducing him to a gaunt figure, his clothes hanging on his dwindling frame.

Justice and Jamal were unwavering in their presence, day in and day out, beside their father's bedside. Every sunrise, they offered silent prayers, and their faces reflected the hope for a miraculous recovery, despite the pain lurking within their hearts that threatened to take over them.

Justice took on an unexpected motherly role, ensuring stability for herself and her younger brother. Even with the truth weighing on her, she remained a source of strength for Jamal. Deep inside, she couldn't ignore the gnawing sense that their father's condition was beyond salvation, that the future was bleaker than they could bear to acknowledge. But she couldn't let her brother see her doubt.

Jamal found himself locked in a battle of optimism. He refused to entertain the thought of his father's death. In the depths of his naivety, he clung to the belief that their father would emerge from this ordeal bigger, and better. His youthful heart refused to accept the grim reality, and he was steady in his denial.

It was a battle between despair and hope, a heartrending melody that underscored their days and nights in that hospital room. As they navigated this journey, the siblings were bound by a shared love for their father and their conflicting emotions, straining against the cruel truth that had taken root within the confines of the hospital walls.

After a year and two months of agonizing decline, Blake's condition had grown even more unbearable. His suffering knew no bounds, and the light of hope had faded into the darkness. Every moment had become a torment, an agony that he could no longer bear. In whispered, raspy words, he pleaded with Justice to end it, to release him from the pain that had consumed his existence.

For weeks, he had begged her, his eyes, once vibrant, now hollow, staring into her soul. And in those pleading eyes, he saw an understanding, a bond between them, a daughter's love for her father. He had watched his children grow, nurtured their dreams, and now, in the most heart-wrenching of roles, he was asking her to grant him mercy.

Justice, burdened by the heaviest decision of her life, felt her world crumble under the weight of her father's suffering. With trembling hands, she gave her consent, a reluctant acknowledgment of the inevitability of this grim choice. Her burden grew heavy, a life's end approaching.

Unplugging life support left a lasting mark on their memories. The machine's sound, once comforting, now seemed ominous. Side by side, they stood, eyes fixed on their father in the hospital bed, the remnants of the man who had personified love and strength for them. The monitor counted down the seconds, each beep of the heart machine marking the diminishing rhythm of their father's life.

Tears streamed as they watched their former protector slip away. Blake Carter had imparted countless jewels of wisdom and life lessons to his children, preparing them for the world they would face. But no preparation could prepare them for this heart-wrenching reality. They bid farewell to the man who had been their cornerstone.

Raw emotions filled the void Blake Carter left behind as the last beep sounded in the room. Despite the cruelest goodbyes, his legacy, love, and impact remain the family's strength.

On the day of Blake's funeral, the entire community was in attendance. The love and respect poured out for a man who left a mark on their lives. The funeral attracted many mourners, whose expressions stood in stark contrast to the vibrant flowers adorning the caskets and lining the pathways.

Justice played a guiding and supporting role for Jamal during this difficult time. Her brother, who had once been a vibrant force, now trembled in the shadows, consumed by his loss. As they approached the gathering, Justice knew she had to be the glue, holding them together in this storm of sorrow.

The funeral was both devastating and beautiful. Blake's legacy, one of love, sacrifice, and wisdom, was in the air, mingling with the sobs and heartfelt condolences of the attendees.

Amidst the crowd of mourners, Justice stepped forward. She spoke, sharing stories and memories, a eulogy that mirrored the love and lessons her father had imparted. She evoked his dedication to family, and the crowd hung on to every word, tears glistening in their eyes as they connected with the depth of her emotions.

Justice's speech painted a vivid picture of Blake's influence, showcasing the love that he had not only given to his family but had radiated out to the entire community. His wisdom, a guiding light in darkness, benefited those privileged to know him.

Apart from their father's older sister, Sheree, who had

arrived to pay her respects, the Carters had few family members. The intimacy of their family unit was a reminder of the irreplaceable void left by Blake's passing. As soon as the casket was lowered into the earth, they were hit by the reality of their loss like a tidle wave.

Jamal, who had held back his grief for so long, now allowed it to flow. He sobbed, the weight of his sorrow clear in his shaking shoulders. Tears, held back for too long, streamed down his face, reflecting his anguish.

The scene at the graveside was a heart-rending tableau. As they said their last farewells to Blake Carter, the community stood in unity, their grief and respect on display to the man who had touched their lives in the most profound of ways.

In the aftermath of their father's passing, Justice faced a daunting challenge. Despite life's struggle, Blake managed the bills and maintained some semblance of order. But, with his sudden absence, the financial burden that cascaded onto Justice was overwhelming.

The mortgage was past due and demanding immediate attention. The threat of the lights being cut off cast a cold, electric unease over their home, while the unpaid water bill was a ticking time bomb, ready to burst. Justice's mind spun like a hamster wheel, racing through an exhausting cycle of desperate thoughts and options.

The barbershop, once a source of salvation, now symbolized frustration and disappointment. The barbers, who had operated with Blake, had stopped paying rent after his passing, a source of contention that had ignited furious arguments between Justice and Blake's business partner, Derrick.

Interests clashed and desperate pleas filled the barbershop.

Justice stood her ground as she confronted Derrick, who had promised to uphold her father's legacy.

"You know what he built here, right?" Justice's voice trembled. "He gave his all to this place, and you were supposed to be included."

Derrick, a man who had a shared vision with Blake, now prioritized financial gain over preserving the legacy. His response was callous. "Justice, you're a kid," he replied. "You don't understand how this works. Business is business, and I've got bills to pay, too."

Justice's frustration was all over her face as her voice grew louder. "My father trusted you to take care of this place and now it's falling apart! This was his dream, and you're just letting it crumble!"

The argument escalated and sparked like an electrical storm. Justice and Derrick stood on opposing sides of a growing divide, one that threatened to swallow the legacy her father had built.

The weight of responsibility, grief, and frustration pressed on Justice, a young woman fighting to preserve her father's memory and hold on to the life he had worked so hard to provide. The stakes were high, and the outcome uncertain as she navigated the terrain of adult responsibilities and broken promises, all in the name of the love she had for her father.

Circumstances left Justice with no choice but to confront a crossroads she had tried to avoid. As the couple of thousand dollars Blake had left behind dwindled, the reality of their situation became clear. The financial strain suffocated her, forcing the most difficult decision of her life.

Justice knew they had to leave behind the modest house they had once called home. It was a place filled with memories of her father, and it pained her to abandon it, but it was now an unaffordable luxury. The once comforting walls now felt like prison bars, a reminder of the dreams that had been shattered.

Jamal, being too young to comprehend the intricacies of their predicament, was left bewildered by their sudden departure. He was adamant about the barbershop, his young heart a raging inferno of anger and confusion. Justice had to inform him of the truth - the barbershop was now involved in dishonest practices. Derrick had betrayed their father's memory.

The Jacob Riis housing projects were nothing like their previous life. It was a notorious place in the city, where hardship was constant. Justice now navigated a world of uncertainty and deprivation. As they moved into their new, cramped quarters, the reality of their descent into a harsher life weighed on her shoulders.

Each night, she prayed to God, clinging to hope for an escape from the consuming madness in their lives. She knew that to change their situation; she had to do more than what she was capable of, but at that moment, the projects were their only refuge.

2

Justice's search for stability and financial security had led her on a harrowing journey, one that had left her feeling defeated and helpless. As she scoured the city for a 9-5 job, the ever-mounting pile of past-due bills haunted her thoughts. They were a reminder of her father's absence and the dire straits they found themselves in.

The initial phases of her job search were nerve-wracking, an uphill battle that seemed impossible to conquer. Justice encountered rejection after rejection, and the job market felt like a battleground where her dreams were casualties of economic strife.

Then, on one fateful day, as she trudged through the crowded streets, a familiar voice called out to her. She turned to see Keisha Beckford, an old friend from high school. Their unexpected encounter was a lifeline thrown to Justice during her journey.

Keisha said she could help Justice secure a job at the call

center where she was employed. Justice's heart swelled with gratitude, and a ray of optimism pierced the dark clouds that had shrouded her life for so long. This was a ray of light in the darkness, a lifeline she had been seeking.

With a new purpose, Justice returned home, eager to share the news with Jamal. He had been struggling with school, losing their father, and his own personal turmoil. Justice couldn't help but smile as she broke the news to her brother, who, despite his own challenges, shared in her joy.

"Guess what, Jamal," she began. "I ran into Keisha today, and she's gonna get me a job at the call center where she works. It's decent pay, and it could be a step in the right direction."

Jamal's face lit up with a mixture of happiness for his sister and the hint of a relieved smile. "That's great, Justice! Finally, some good news for us."

Justice's two months at the call center had been an exhausting ordeal. The stress that filled the environment was suffocating, and the meager pay made the hardship unbearable. On top of it all, her manager's inappropriate advances had been the final straw. Justice knew that she couldn't endure such a toxic environment any longer.

After much contemplation, Justice made the tough decision to quit. She expressed her gratitude to Keisha for the opportunity, but she couldn't sacrifice her self-respect for a job that had become a nightmare. She was determined to find something else, even if it meant returning to the grueling job hunt.

Back at square one, with no job, the stress of their financial situation closed in on Justice once more. Each day seemed like a challenge, and the search for employment felt like an endless uphill battle. The weight of her responsibilities and the desire to provide for Jamal remained her driving force, but the hurdles they faced seemed insurmountable.

After a long, grueling day of job searching and the feeling of coming up empty-handed, Justice walked back to their project apartment, her shoulders slumped with exhaustion and her spirit weighed down by disappointment. The apartment complex, with its dim hallways, peeling paint and horrid stench of urine felt as bleak as her situation.

With each step she took, the pit in her stomach deepened. As she approached her front door, her heart raced, knowing that the mounting financial pressures might have reached a breaking point. And there, taped to the chipped paint of their front door, was a white envelope, and in it was an eviction notice.

The tears welled up in her eyes as she snatched the piece of paper off the door. The notice was a declaration of their desperate situation. With the weight of the world on her back, a deep sense of helplessness washed over her.

Justice stood there in the hallway, the notice crumpled in her hand, as the reality of their predicament settled in. The apartment, with its peeling paint and flickering overhead light, seemed to close in on her, mirroring the suffocating feeling of desperation that gripped her.

In the kitchen of their project apartment, Justice stood by the stove, the sizzling sound of water coming to a boil filling the air. The humble meal of Chicken Ramen noodles was the best she could muster to ensure that Jamal had something to eat.

Justice's mind drifted back to the days when their father was alive. Blake was the pillar of strength and love in their family, and they had enjoyed the ritual of weekend outings to fancy restaurants. His favorites, the succulent filet mignon and tender lobster tails. Sundays, too, had been special, with Blake donning the role of a master chef, crafting exquisite meals to bring his loved ones together.

But now, as Justice stared at the pot of boiling water, the reality of their situation weighed on her. Their financial struggles had reached a point of desperation, forcing her to pawn most of her jewelry. The small token of her sixteenth birthday, a necklace from her father, remained around her neck. It was a reminder of the bond they shared. In a desperate bid to make ends meet, she sold off everything else, from her designer clothes to her cherished designer bags.

It was a trying time for Justice and Jamal. Their world turned upside down, and Justice shouldered the burden of shielding her younger brother from the harsh realities that threatened to crush their dreams. Jamal was determined to focus on school, but even in the classroom, his grades were waning, a reflection of the turmoil that had infiltrated their lives.

As the hardships continued to multiply, Justice remained undeterred in her search for employment. The job hunt had taken on an air of desperation, and she was willing to take any job that would provide financial relief. She had even considered returning to the call center, but to her dismay, all the positions were filled.

The mounting rejections in her job search had become a constant, demoralizing force, threatening to erode her sense of self-worth. Each "no" was a painful reminder of the battle she faced, and it wore on her like an unbearable weight.

Amid their dire circumstances, Justice wrestled with thoughts of drastic measures, contemplating actions she had never considered. The continuous rejection and the growing feeling of desperation had stripped away her self-confidence, leaving her feeling diminished and uncertain about the future.

Standing in the waiting room of the welfare office, a place she had never imagined herself being, Justice's eyes swept across the sea of faces that mirrored her own. The room overflowed with society's struggles, humbly reminding Justice of the countless individuals who had been brought to their knees by circumstances beyond their control.

The feeling of humiliation gnawed at her as she navigated this unfamiliar territory. It was a place she never thought she would find herself, and it left her with a sense of vulnerability and frustration. Seeking help from local charities and food banks had already required putting her pride aside, and now, in the government assistance office, that sense of frustration was magnified.

Justice's goal was to secure income for her family. The weight of her embarrassment and frustration pressed on her shoulders, but she had reached a point where her commitment to her brother's well-being had taken precedence over her pride.

Faced with mounting difficulties, Justice was determined to guide Jamal, emphasizing the importance of his education and how he presented himself to the world. However, Jamal, now in his junior year at Lincoln High School, was marching to the beat of his own drum. His grades had plummeted to a dismal array of D's and F's, and he had undergone a shift in his attitude. The quiet boy was fading, giving way to a more assertive, independent persona, both on the streets and at home.

One evening, after returning from her job hunt, Justice discovered a letter from Jamal's school in the mail. The words on the paper were a crushing blow: Jamal was failing all of his classes, and he was on the verge of being kicked off the swim team. The news felt impossible to digest. She thought she must have misread it. Not Jamal.

Overwhelmed by disbelief, Justice sought her brother, who was lounging in the living room, flipping through television channels. "Jamal," she called out. "Can you explain this?" She held up the letter, her eyes fixed on his.

Jamal stared back at his sister, his nonchalant demeanor suggesting that nothing was wrong. "Jamal, do you hear me talking to you?"

"Yes, Justice, I hear you," he replied, feigning indifference.

"Then explain this," Justice pressed.

"Explain what?" Jamal evaded the topic.

Justice's frustration surged. "Jamal, you're failing all your classes, and you're about to be kicked off the swim team. What's going on with you?" Her voice carried a mixture of concern and frustration.

"I ain't feeling that school anymore," Jamal admitted. "And I'm done with swimming. That shit is for pussies."

The words struck Justice like a punch to the gut, and she struggled to maintain her composure. "Watch your mouth, Jamal," she warned him.

"Or what, Justice? I'm not a kid anymore. You can't tell me what to do."

Justice stared at her younger brother, and for a moment, time seemed to hang suspended between them. His assertion still lingered in the air: he was no longer a child, and that fact was becoming more evident by the day. But for Justice, Jamal would always be her little brother, a fact that ran far deeper than age.

She could see a transformation taking place within him, one that extended beyond the physical changes he was undergoing. His character, his essence, was evolving, shifting, and growing in ways she couldn't have predicted. As an older sister, she recognized the importance of letting him find his own path and make his own choices, even though it felt like her world was changing too fast.

But, on this evening, after a long day filled with struggles, Justice was too tired to engage in an argument that was going nowhere. She needed to pick her battles carefully, especially when it came to Jamal, who had been through so much. Her heart ached for her brother, and she didn't want him to feel abandoned.

With a resigned tone, she spoke, "You're right." She paused for a moment, collecting her thoughts. "And I don't want to argue about it. But you're better than this, Jamal, and you know it." Her words were both an acknowledgment of his independence and a reminder of the potential she saw in him.

Jamal exhaled and gave his sister a subtle nod of understanding. The unspoken complexities of their relationship and the challenges they faced hung in the air, but they remained bound by their shared experiences and the love that connected them as family.

A knock at the door startled both Justice and Jamal from their conversation. Justice hurried over and peeked through the peephole, revealing their neighbor Pamela. She greeted her with a warm smile as she undid the locks and opened the door. "Hey, how you doing, Ms. Pam?" Justice inquired, holding the door wide open.

Wasting no time, Pamela got straight to the point. "Neighbor, mi need fi borrow twenty dolla until di number one day of di month. Please, neighbor. Mi likkle yoot dem can't eat. Please," she implored.

Justice's heart went out to her neighbor. She knew Ms. Pam had three children and was raising them all by herself. She couldn't ignore the empathy she felt for Ms. Pam, even though money was tight in their own household. As she pondered the situation, Justice realized everyone had their own share of difficulties and battles to confront.

With a sense of understanding, Justice reached into her pocket and produced a five-dollar bill. "Here," she said, passing the money to Ms. Pam. "This is all I can spare right now. But wait here for a moment. I'll be right back."

Justice disappeared into the kitchen and returned with a box of oatmeal. She handed it to Ms. Pam with a warm smile. "Here, this should help."

"Thank you! Mi so grateful fi have you as mi neighbor. Bless," Pamela replied, her gratitude clear in her voice.

After a few more weeks of job hunting, Justice landed a job at a fast-food restaurant. Her new role was the night manager, and it provided her with some hope during their financial struggles. And just when it seemed like things might be looking up, Justice received a callback for a second job as a mail courier in the city. With these two sources of income combined, she could at least keep her and Jamal afloat, even though things were still tight.

One evening, as Justice worked through her shift at the restaurant, a sleek burgundy Mercedes Benz pulled up to the drive-through window. The dark tinted glass slid down, and Justice's eyes widened as she recognized her longtime friend, Keisha Beckford, behind the wheel.

"Keisha? Is that you?" Justice's face broke into a wide smile as she greeted her old friend.

Keisha turned toward the voice, and when her eyes met Justice's, her face lit up with surprise and delight. "Justice! Damn, girl, it's been too long!" Keisha leaned out of the window, extending a hand in a friendly wave.

Justice nodded, juggling her responsibilities behind the counter as she conversed with her friend. "Tell me about it. I've been swamped with work. Still remember our call center days, though."

Keisha sucked her teeth and rolled her eyes. "Call center, huh? I'm living a whole different life now."

Justice couldn't help but admire Keisha's luxurious Benz. She knew it was an expensive vehicle. She couldn't resist inquiring, "How'd you get this car?"

Keisha's eyes sparkled with mischief as she leaned closer to the window. "Girl, everything's changed. My brother's home now. But I don't want to spill all the tea through this tiny drive-through window. What time you get off?"

Justice checked the time on her phone. "Another hour to go. Why?"

Keisha grinned. "I'll be back to pick you up when your shift is over. We got some catching up to do. And don't forget to grab some of those biscuits. I've been craving them!"

They shared a chuckle, their laughter a reminder of the friendship that had endured over the years.

An hour later, Justice clocked out of her shift and made her way over to Keisha's waiting Mercedes Benz. As she opened the passenger door and settled into the plush leather seat, the car's luxurious interior caught her eye. It reminded her of her late father's car, the very Benz he had cherished.

Keisha broke the silence, "So, what's going on, girl?"

Justice sighed, her weariness clear in her voice. "Just working and trying to keep the lights on, you know? Bills piling up faster than I can make the money to pay 'em." Justice couldn't help but turn her gaze to the elegant interior of the car. "What's the deal with this car, Keisha?"

Keisha leaned back. "I was getting to that. My brother's back home. You remember my little brother, right?"

Justice ransacked her memories, then her eyes widened as she recalled. "Lucian, right?"

Keisha nodded, flashing a smile. "That's him. Lucian, but now he goes by Luck. He just came home after doing five years in the feds. But let me tell you, he's back on top."

Justice, still puzzled, inquired, "Back on top? What you mean?"

Keisha lit a blunt and the pungent aroma of marijuana smoke filled the car's interior. "Yup," she said, exhaling slowly. "Luck. He's one of the top dogs in these streets. Him and his crew pull in serious paper, and since he came home, he's been lookin' out for me and the family, you know, taking care of us."

Justice was surprised by Keisha's revelation. *Her friend's brother was involved in the street life?* It was a world she knew nothing about. As Keisha passed the blunt, the intrigue of the situation drew her in.

"You smoke?" Keisha asked, her eyes locking on Justice as she held out the blunt.

Justice stared at the offered blunt, contemplating the decision that lay before her. She had always been careful about her choices and had never indulged in any form of drug use. Her father's words played back in her mind, *"Drugs are the shortcuts that lead to dead ends."* But now, she was faced with an unexpected situation.

However, her friendship with Keisha was different. They had been through a lot together and shared their joys and sorrows. She didn't want to offend her friend or create an awkward situation. She knew Keisha was well-aware of her clean record, and her offer was a gesture of trust. Justice convinced herself that she couldn't let her friend down or make her feel uncomfortable.

She reached out and accepted the blunt, her voice laced with a hint of playfulness. "I am today," Justice said, taking the blunt from Keisha's hand. Inhaling, she allowed the smoke to fill her lungs.

The pungent aroma and the sensation of the smoke were strange to her, but she didn't want to show any signs of discomfort. It was her way of showing that she could adapt, just as her life had forced her to adapt to challenging circumstances. As the room seemed to take on a different hue, Justice's mind wandered, and she braced herself for the forthcoming conversation about Keisha's brother and their involvement in the dangerous world of the streets.

Justice watched Keisha with a mix of curiosity and disbelief. The world Keisha was describing was far from her own reality. She inhaled the remnants of the smoke that lingered in the car's interior and met Keisha's gaze. "So, what does Lucian do?" Justice questioned, passing the blunt back to her friend. The thought of Keisha's brother being involved in criminal activities seemed surreal to her.

Keisha took another hit of the blunt, leaned back in her seat, and let out a plume of thick smoke before responding. "He does a bit of everything. His main thing is robberies."

Justice's brows furrowed. Robberies? The word hung in the air. "You're involved in... robberies?" She asked, a tinge of disbelief in her voice.

Keisha grinned, unfazed by the surprise in Justice's eyes. "Nah, not me, per se. I handle the scouting for that. My main hustle is check fraud."

Justice was taken aback. She found herself at the edge of a world she had never imagined. Keisha's casual tone as she described these illegal activities sent shivers down Justice's spine. She couldn't help but wonder if her newfound friend would drag her deeper into this dark world.

As the night settled, Justice and Keisha remained cocooned in the sleek Mercedes Benz, the car's interior awash in the glow of the streetlights. The scent of the marijuana lingered, mingling with the tension that hung in the air.

For over two hours, Keisha had recounted her life and the lucrative endeavors she was a part of. She spoke of wealth and money, numbers so vast that Justice couldn't fathom them. The enormity of Keisha's world had consumed her dreams. Justice couldn't help but feel a mixture of awe and dread as she contemplated the offers her friend had made.

Keisha pulled up in front of the Jacob Riis housing projects. Justice climbed out of the luxurious vehicle, her emotions tangled like a complex web. She looked at Keisha, grateful but burdened by the choices that lay ahead. She was thankful for the opportunity Keisha had presented but torn by the realization that it would defy her father's teachings.

Life was unraveling, and it was moving fast. As she stood under the streetlight, Justice knew she faced a hell of a decision, one that could pull her deeper into a world she had never imagined.

She turned to Keisha. "Thank you for everything. I'll see you on the agreed date. I need some time to think, but I appreciate the chance."

With that, they bid each other farewell, and Justice retreated into the pitch blackness of the housing projects, weighed down by the gravity of the choices she would soon have to make. The darkness swallowed her, but her path remained uncertain.

In the days leading up to the meeting, Justice was more nervous than ever before. The promise of a life where she and Jamal could live had shaken her focus, casting a web of distraction over her daily routine. At work, her mind wandered as she envisioned the wealth that was just within reach.

But, as the hours ticked away and the day of the meeting approached, Justice fought with her principles. She was resolute in her decision not to cross certain moral boundaries, no matter the sum of money dangled before her.

When Keisha's text message came on the designated day, it provided the address and time for the meeting. Without hesitation, Justice made her way to the location, a cathedral church nestled in the heart of downtown Manhattan. She realized it was an odd choice for a meeting, but she was willing to trust in the path she had chosen.

Under the glow of the streetlights, Justice stood near the cathedral, awaiting a sign of Keisha's arrival. The grand facade of the church loomed behind her, an imposing presence that seemed to mirror the gravity of the decisions that lay ahead. The meeting was fast approaching, and Justice could feel the tension coiling in her gut as she prepared to step into an unknown world.

After a few minutes of waiting, Justice caught a glimpse of

Keisha's burgundy Mercedes pulling up to the curb. The sight of her friend brought relief. Keisha stepped out of the car and gestured for Justice to follow.

Justice fell in step as they made their way into the cathedral. The grandeur of the church was nothing short of awe-inspiring; its vast interior had low lighting, a place of solemnity and quiet reflection. Their footsteps sounded in the hushed stillness as they ventured deeper into the space.

Justice had never set foot inside a cathedral before, and the sheer scale of the place took her breath away. The high vaulted ceilings, the ornate stained glass windows, and the towering stone pillars all left her feeling insignificant in the face of such majesty.

As they continued to traverse the cathedral's depths, Justice's eyes fell on a group of people who had gathered at the back of a pew. The sight of the congregation only deepened the sense of reverence and apprehension, and she couldn't help but feel like an outsider stepping into a sacred realm. But the meeting would thrust her into a world she could never have imagined, and she prepared herself for what lay ahead.

Keisha and Justice approached the group. As they drew closer, a tall man in a well-fitted suit, sporting a full beard and dark shades, stepped forward, obstructing their path. Keisha, unbothered by his presence, waved her hand before a light he held, allowing herself to pass through.

"Miss Beckford," he said, allowing her entrance. But when Justice tried to follow, she was stopped.

Keisha interjected, attempting to vouch for her friend. "She's with me."

"She has to be searched." He told her.

Justice maintained her composure, although she was flustered by the sudden intrusion on her privacy. The suited man directed her to lift her arms, and then proceeded with a meticulous pat-down, ensuring there were no concealed weapons. The process felt invasive.

Keisha, growing agitated by the situation, vented her frustration with a few choice words. "This is some bullshit!"

However, a deep voice from the shadows nearby offered a reminder of the necessity for discretion. "Rules must be obeyed, sister."

Keisha turned her head to find her brother, Luck, hidden in the dark. His presence signaling that adherence to the rules was paramount in this world.

As Luck stepped out of the shadows and embraced his sister, the surrounding atmosphere radiated authority and danger. He held her with an air of confidence that showcased his dominance in this world. His eyes, however, shifted from Keisha to Justice, like a predator assessing fresh prey. She was standing there, innocent as ever. He could see it. She didn't belong there. But she was the most beautiful woman he'd ever seen in his life. Her eyes were curious and apprehensive, and her presence exuded a sense of purity.

Keisha could feel the energy between the two of them. It was radiating. She broke the silence. "Lucian," she said. "This is Justice, Justice, my brother Lucian, but everyone here calls him Luck."

Luck extended his arm to shake Justice's hand. Her skin was soft. "Pleasure to meet you," he said, his voice smooth and polite, masking the aura of power that surrounded him.

Lucian, or Luck, as he's known on the streets, had just served five years in the federal penitentiary. He was a commanding figure, standing at a towering 6 feet, 3 inches. He had shaved his face, showcasing chiseled features and a pair of calculating eyes that seemed to miss nothing. His smiled revealed bright white teeth, which only added to his charisma.

Luck's background had its roots in a tough neighborhood, where he learned to navigate the terrain with street smarts and a heart as cold as ice. Establishing himself as a natural leader, he rose to prominence as the head of one of the most notorious robbery crews in the country. He was no stranger to audacious heists that made headlines, leading to his eventual downfall and a five-year prison sentence.

However, prison was just another chapter in his life. During his incarceration, Luck used the time to sharpen his criminal mind and expand his network. He recruited like-minded individuals and solidified his reputation as a strategic thinker. He lived by a simple but powerful mantra: "Money, Power, Respect." These three words guided his every move.

Upon his release, Luck was determined to regain his status. His charisma and intelligence made him a magnet for those seeking wealth and influence. Many women were attracted to his charm, but few could escape the danger concealed behind his smile.

Now back on the streets, Luck's presence sent ripples through the criminal underworld. He had already reclaimed his position at the top, and anyone who crossed his path would feel the weight of his power.

Justice's hand tingled as Luck's firm grip enveloped it. She couldn't look away from his piercing eyes. His voice, smooth and commanding, held an irresistible magnetism.

"You ready to indulge in this lifestyle?" Luck's words held the weight of their potential consequences. Justice locked eyes with him, the intensity of the moment almost suffocating. She felt a strange connection to this dangerous way of living he represented.

"As long as you're the one guiding me..." she answered. Justice had taken her first step into a world that was a far cry from anything she had ever known. She cast the die, setting her destiny in motion.

❧ 3 ☙

Justice stepped out of the luxurious car, her heart thumping in her chest. It was the beginning of her walk onto the other side, and it was far from glamorous. The rendezvous had been brief. Luck handed her an envelope. "This is part of your initiation," he had told her. "Let's see if you built for this shit."

As she stood on the corner, holding the envelope, she sensed a combination of excitement and apprehension. She realized that once she entered this world, there would be no going back. Justice looked around at the abandoned buildings, the distant sirens, and the graffiti-covered walls. She thought of Jamal back in their small apartment, oblivious to the choices she was making. The contents of the envelope reminded her she was doing this for him, or so she told herself. Justice was unable to avoid wondering what her father's response would be if he had the chance to witness her current situation, if he possessed knowledge of the route she was exploring.

A car idled by the curb, its windows tinted almost black. The driver nodded toward her. "You got that?" he asked, his voice gruff and demanding. She nodded back, confirming that she had the package. This was the moment she had to decide, a decision that would shape her future. Justice leaned into the car's open window, passing the envelope off to someone she didn't know, and had never seen. She wasn't even aware of the contents in the envelope. Her presence was purely for the job.

The car pulled away, fading into the night, and Justice felt a knot in her stomach. She was now caught up in something bigger and darker than she could have imagined. She began her journey into street crime, encountering unexpected challenges and dilemmas.

In just one week, Justice had made it through the initiation phase, proving herself in the world Luck had introduced her to. The jitters faded as she adapted to new rules and expectations.

As she got dressed, her eyes kept drifting to the stack of cash she had earned during that first week. Five thousand dollars, crisp and bundled. The amount was life-changing for Justice, who had modest means growing up. She couldn't help but think about the bills, debt, and struggles they could overcome with this money. But the allure of wealth came at a price she was realizing.

In the tiny living room of their project apartment, Justice found Jamal sitting on the worn-out sofa, his schoolbooks scattered in front of him. She hesitated for a moment, observing her younger brother's dedication to his studies, even during their hardships. She knew she had to support him, to offer him a better future. "Jamal," she said, her voice soft yet resolute, "I need to go out for a while, but I left you some money for food."

The look of surprise and gratitude in Jamal's eyes was priceless. "Thank you, Justice," he replied, taking the money without questions.

With a deep breath, Justice grabbed her bag. After locking the door, she headed to the subway, aware that her choices would reshape her life, and she was hoping to make the right ones.

Stepping out of the subway terminal, Justice spotted Keisha's car. The sight of the familiar Mercedes offered her some reassurance, but as she got into the backseat, her nerves returned. A mysterious man sat in the front passenger seat, his features hidden beneath dark shades and a hoodie. He never turned to acknowledge her presence, adding to the ominous atmosphere inside the vehicle.

Keisha wasted no time. She leaned back to address Justice. "Listen to me," she began, her tone serious. "There's a black BMW parked a block over from here. Here's the key. The GPS on the phone that's in that car will take you to where you need to go."

As Keisha handed her the key, Justice couldn't help but notice the seriousness in her friend's voice and demeanor. Justice's intuition was shouting at her that something significant was about to happen. She was prepared for some level of danger, but her heart skipped a beat as Keisha continued.

"Justice, there's thirty bricks in that car," Keisha disclosed, her eyes locking onto Justice's. Those words hit her like a sledgehammer. *Thirty bricks.* The enormity of the situation struck her, and a surge of anxiety pulsed through her. *What had she gotten herself into?*

Justice knew there was no turning back. Realizing the need to focus on her entrusted mission, each passing day added complexity to her life in this new world.

Justice sat in the driver's seat of the BMW, struggling with the gravity of the situation. The iPhone in the car's console lit up, revealing a long-distance destination of 400 miles on the GPS. She would arrive in the city of Lynchburg, Virginia, in seven hours. Doubt crept into her mind, and she questioned the life she had chosen. Her heartbeat quickened, and she wondered if this world she was entering was worth the cost.

Then, the thought of Jamal cut through the fog of uncertainty. The determination to secure her brother's future and provide him with a better life was all she could think of. This was her path now, a choice she couldn't back out of. She readied herself and took a deep breath.

Before starting the car, she examined the interior, searching for any sign of the thirty bricks. Her doubts whispered that perhaps this was all a test, that she wasn't expected to transport such an enormous load. Her inspection revealed only the expected items—paperwork, the phone, and nothing more. It was a curious situation.

Just as Justice was about to ignite the engine, the iPhone rang, startling her. She answered, hearing Keisha's voice on the other end. "Hello?"

Keisha's instructions came across the line. "Justice, reach up under the seat. There's something there for you," she said. Justice followed her friend's directions, her hand disappearing under the driver's seat. Her fingers met cold, hard steel. She retrieved the weapon, staring at it in her hand.

Justice had never held a gun before, and it felt alien, yet a sense of empowerment washed over her. She hesitated but, under Keisha's watchful voice, broke free from her trance. "Uh… yeah, I'm good," she responded. "Getting ready to pull off."

Keisha's voice held a warning in its tone. "That's there for a reason. If you ever need to use it, don't hesitate," she cautioned. "I'll be in contact." And with that, she hung up.

With the pistol now resting beside her, Justice started the car, her mind fixed on the drive ahead and the shifting nature of her life, so far from the familiar world she had once known.

As she cruised down the highway, the weight of her choices weighed on her, and anxiety clawed at her thoughts. She couldn't escape the unease that settled in her stomach, growing with each passing mile.

Her grip on the steering wheel tightened as she imagined flashing red and blue lights in her rearview mirror. Beads of sweat formed on her forehead, and her trembling hands caused the car to sway. She knew that getting pulled over could be disastrous.

Desperation and fear waged a battle inside of her. She rolled down all the windows, allowing the cool night air to rush in, providing some clarity. The rush of wind helped her focus on the task at hand and pushed away the rising doubts.

Justice was aware that her father, wherever he was now, would disapprove of her actions. The memory of his lessons, his love for them, poked on her conscience. She envisioned his disappointed face, and it pained her.

But she also knew that there was no one left to care for her and Jamal except herself. She had to make tough choices for their survival. The knowledge that her family's future hung in the balance gave her the strength to persist.

She repeated a mantra in her mind: "No reward without the risk." It was time to step it up.

As Justice whispered her mantra, her eyes went to the rearview mirror and found their reflection in the blue and red flashing lights that painted the dark highway behind her. The wailing sirens grew louder, and with each approaching second, her heart dropped to her feet.

Fear constricted her chest, making it hard to breathe. She knew that in the glove compartment, she had the documents—insurance and registration—the officer would request. But her thoughts shifted to what she kept under the driver's seat.

The unregistered .40 caliber lay there, a cold, silent menace, taunting her as the police cruiser pulled up behind her car. Panic washed over her as she remembered the "thirty bricks" that were supposed to be in the car. She could feel the beads of sweat trickling down the side of her face. A voice in her head shouted that she had to stay calm.

Justice reached into the glove compartment, fumbling with the paperwork she needed. Her nerves were a mess, and she hoped the officer wouldn't sense her anxiety.

The fear intensified as the State Trooper's boots crunched on the gravel. His uniform was dark against the highway lights. Her mind raced through various scenarios. If she couldn't locate the thirty bricks, maybe the police wouldn't either.

She locked eyes with her reflection in the rearview mirror again, watching the officer's approach. The seconds ticked away like an eternity. All she could think about was that gun underneath her seat.

State Trooper Malinowski, a lanky Caucasian man, made his way to the driver's side door with deliberate, methodical movements. He gripped his flashlight tight, ready for whatever awaited him. With a deft motion, he withdrew the flashlight and shone a piercing light into the car's interior, scanning for anything suspicious. The beam of the flashlight danced across the dashboard, the seats, and the shadows beneath.

Tap, tap, tap — he rapped the back of the flashlight against the window pane. "License and registration, Ma'am," he requested when Justice rolled down her window. He could sense her nervousness in the air.

Taking the proffered documents, he examined them, scrutinizing each word and number, the gears turning in his head. His eyes moved up from the documents to study Justice's anxious face. "Sit tight, I'll be right back," he told her, not giving away any of his thoughts.

Justice sat still, beads of sweat forming on her brow. With each passing moment, the discomfort grew more profound. Doubts and fears consumed her.

The officer returned in what felt like an eternity to Justice. He handed the documents back to her with an air of indifference. Then he leaned closer to the driver's window, his gaze shifting past her towards the interior of the vehicle. His words, cordial yet probing. "This here's a nice car you're driving. Where you coming from?"

Justice inhaled, doing her best to suppress her rising anxiety. "New York, sir," she replied, her voice quivering.

The trooper stepped towards the back of the car and directed his attention to the out-of-state license plate. "We get a lot of folks trafficking drugs passing through here with those out-of-state plates. You ain't got no drugs in this car, do you?"

Justice's throat went dry as she swallowed hard. "No, sir," she responded.

Then came the pivotal question that could determine her fate. "You mind if I search the vehicle?"

She had only a fraction of a moment to weigh her options. She'd seen enough cop shows to know what could happen if she refused. The consequences could be dire, even if there was nothing incriminating in her car. A slow, hesitant nod signaled her compliance. "Sure, officer. No problem."

The trooper's visage remained stoic, and he issued a directive in that cool, authoritative manner. "Good. Step out of the vehicle and stand over here."

Justice exhaled, the tension clear in every movement as she unbuckled her seatbelt and emerged from the car, her footsteps taking her to the designated spot by the side of the road. The encounter had just taken a treacherous turn, and Justice could feel the weight of the choices she'd made bearing down on her.

Trooper Malinowski's flashlight darted around the vehicle's interior, probing every nook and cranny. Justice's anxiety was obvious, the seconds stretching into what felt like hours. Her eyes stayed glued to the unfolding scene, and she crossed her fingers, praying that her secret cargo remained undiscovered.

The beam of the flashlight danced over the passenger side, then over the backseat. Beads of sweat continued to gather on Justice's forehead, her eyes wide and unblinking as she watched the trooper's every move. The worst-case scenarios swirled in her mind as she feared the consequences of being caught.

As the trooper moved towards the driver's side, her heart raced in her chest. He continued to flash the light around, inspecting every corner of the car, and then, in a heart-stopping moment, he reached beneath the driver's seat.

Justice held her breath, the world narrowing down to that solitary moment. Every instinct screamed at her, and then the trooper's hand emerged from beneath the seat, empty. The flood of relief that went through her was clear, and she let out the breath she hadn't realized she was holding. The gun had remained hidden, at least for now.

As the trooper concluded his search, he delivered the verdict that she had been hoping for. "Okay, Ma'am. Looks like you're all clean. Drive safe."

Justice barely mumbled a tense, "Thank you," as the state trooper retreated to his patrol car. It was only when his vehicle pulled away that Justice allowed herself to take a shaky, deep breath. She looked up at the sky, feeling a mix of gratitude and anxiety, realizing how close she had come to the edge. With a surge of adrenaline, she rushed back to the driver's seat and started the car, determined to continue on her route, a little wiser and more cautious.

Justice had been driving for hours, her tension never dissipating after her encounter with the state trooper. Her eyes were weary from the road, and her muscles ached from hours of gripping the steering wheel. Finally, the exit she had been awaiting came into view.

As she exited the highway, her heart raced. She answered her iPhone when it rang, and Keisha's voice came through. "Hello?" she responded.

"You're half an hour late. What happened?" Keisha's voice was sharp, reflecting the impatience of the situation.

Justice tried to soothe her friend's concerns. "I got pulled over in New Jersey by a state trooper."

"Oh. Well, if I'm talking to you, everything must be good," Keisha replied, a hint of relief in her voice.

Justice exhaled. "Yes. Everything is good. They searched the car and didn't find anything." Justice's tone shifted. "Is that stuff really in this car?" She paused for a moment, emphasizing the weight of the cargo they were transporting.

"You're asking too many questions, Justice. Just do as you're told. Now, when you pull up to the spot, they'll handle everything with the car. But Justice…" Keisha's voice dropped low. "Don't leave VA without the money."

"What money?" she questioned, panic creeping into her voice.

Keisha's tone was stern. "There should be seven hundred and fifty thousand in two duffle bags. Make sure you get those bags, Justice. Don't come back without them." With those last words, Keisha hung up.

The weight of her words settled over Justice. *Seven hundred and fifty thousand dollars.* It was an unimaginable sum, and the responsibility for obtaining it weighed on her shoulders. Her entire life had changed in such a short time, and she couldn't help but wonder how her father, a man who had instilled in her a sense of integrity and hard work, would view the choices she had made. But for Jamal, she would continue on this path, determined to secure a future for him that held promise and hope.

Justice parked the BMW in the parking garage at the given address. Before she opened the car door and stepped out, she reached underneath the seat, grabbed the gun and placed it on her waistline like she had seen in videos. Her eyes landed on two men who were waiting for her. One was tall, his dark skin contrasting with long dreadlocks that reached down his back. The other, shorter but stocky, with a head full of waves.

Easy and Loc had a reputation in the drug trade on the streets of Lynchburg, VA. Easy, with his stocky build and waves of thick, black hair, held an air of menace that belied his relaxed demeanor. He was a short, powerful force known for his quick thinking, which made him a dangerous ally and an even more dangerous adversary.

Loc was a towering presence with long, dark dreadlocks cascading down his back. He was the boisterous one, obnoxious and full of himself. His impulsive nature made him the perfect counterpart to Easy's calculating tendencies. Together, they formed a dynamic partnership that was feared by many on the streets where they thrived.

Justice knew they were assessing the situation and her presence, sizing her up. Loc spoke first. "Ahh, I see this dude got smart, huh?" His words suggested they were familiar with Luck's associates. Justice maintained her composure, not giving away her nervousness or irritation.

"He be using them niggas who don't know any better," he continued, his eyes scanning the BMW's interior. "But he switched it up, went wit' a bitch this time." The derogatory comment about her being Luck's *"bitch"* stung, but she remained silent, unwilling to give him the satisfaction of a reaction.

"Don't worry," he continued with a smirk, "we'll take care of this." He gestured towards the car, implying that they would handle transporting whatever was inside. "It'll take about an hour. You can wait here or sit at the kitchen table while we get this sorted."

Justice hesitated for a moment, caught between her unease and the realization that she had little choice but to follow through. She considered what was at stake and the path she had chosen, a path filled with risk and danger.

She waited while the two men dismantled the BMW. As they extracted the wrapped packages concealed within the car's interior paneling, Justice was in shock. It was real; the drugs were in the car. She recalled the amount of money involved and understood that she was entangled in something far beyond her prior experience.

The men completed their task, counting the packages, ensuring nothing was missing. When Loc claimed that one package was missing, laughter erupted between them, but it was an eerie humor that only intensified Justice's anxiety. As she watched them, her heart raced, and she couldn't help but imagine all the ways things could go wrong.

They confirmed everything was in order, and Loc gestured to a small table in the corner where a key rested. Justice seized the key and made her way to the return car parked outside. The sum of seven hundred and fifty thousand dollars played in her mind like a warning.

With trembling hands, she popped open the trunk, only to find it empty. Panic shot through her entire body. Keisha's voice replayed in her head, insisting she return with the money. In this tense moment, doubt and fear consumed her. *Did they leave the bags out? Or had she misunderstood the instructions?* Justice fought to calm herself, determined to find a way forward in this dangerous world she had entered.

The tension in the room had reached its peak as Justice confronted the two men, seeking answers about the missing bags. Her pleas fell on deaf ears, and their dismissal turned into a threat.

Unsure of what was going on, Justice felt trapped, cornered in a situation she didn't comprehend. But the words from Keisha, *"Don't come back without those bags,"* echoed in her mind, urging her to make a choice.

In a desperate move, Justice reached for the gun concealed in her waistband and pointed it at the two men.

Loc responded, "Bitch, what the fuck you gon' do wit' that?"

But Justice couldn't let fear hold her back. Her life depended on it.

With trembling hands, she squeezed the trigger, only to hear an empty click. Her heart filled with terror and confusion as she struggled to figure out the unfamiliar weapon. Then, the memory of a movie surfaced in her mind—she needed to pull the gun back to chamber a bullet.

Justice adjusted the firearm, loading a round into the chamber. She hesitated for just a moment, aware of the danger surrounding her. When she fired, the gun erupted, unleashing a rapid succession of shots.

Bullets cut through the air. Easy dove for cover, and got hit, while Loc reached for his own weapon, but it was too late. Justice continued to squeeze the trigger until the gun clicked empty. The gunfire ceased, leaving behind a chilling silence.

Afraid to move, Justice emerged from her cover, scanning the room. Her eyes fell on the two bodies sprawled on the kitchen floor, pools of blood forming around them. In a matter of seconds, her world had turned from confusion and fear into a scene of cold, stark murder.

The weight of her actions sank in, leaving her standing there, shaken and overwhelmed.

Justice found herself in a surreal scene, standing over the bodies, still gripping the hot gun in her hands. She struggled to grasp the gravity of her actions. Blood pooled around the two men, their faces forever frozen in expressions of shock and surprise.

Shaken from her stupor, Justice realized she had to locate the missing bags. She searched the room, hoping they had been overlooked. With desperation driving her, she scoured every hiding place, from cabinets to the refrigerator. Her efforts yielded nothing, and panic crept in.

An urge drove her back to the garage, the stripped BMW serving as a reminder of the high-stakes world she had entered. In a corner, she spotted two duffle bags, unzipping one to find stacks of money tumbling out. Justice snatched both bags, holding on tight to the fruits of her labor.

But her mission was not complete. As she rushed back into the house, she left nothing behind. She grabbed two black garbage bags from the cabinet and packed every kilo she could find.

Once she had the duffle bags with the $750,000 and the two garbage bags containing 30 bricks, Justice hesitated. Fear gnawed at her, but she had come too far to turn back now. With one last glance at the scene, she closed the door and fled, jumping into the return car and speeding off down the highway.

The weight of her decisions, the lives she had disrupted, and the imminent dangers she faced all swirled in her mind as the road stretched out before her. Justice found herself thrust into a treacherous game where survival demanded quick thinking, ruthless actions, and a bitter heart to protect her family.

Tears welled in her eyes as she pulled over to the side of the highway, unable to contain the turmoil inside of her. The scene of violence and death replayed in her mind like a nightmare. Understanding the impact of taking not one, but two lives weighed heavily on her conscience, and the guilt gnawed at her soul.

In that lonely moment, she found relief by herself in the car, embracing the steering wheel, her body convulsing with each sob. Her whispered prayers for forgiveness, her pleas for guidance, and the memories of her father filled the quiet space. She hoped that he would be able to understand the desperate choices she had been forced to make.

After her emotional release, Justice wiped her tears and got herself together. She was aware that remaining in this place of sorrow was not an option. Her father's spirit seemed to offer a silent understanding, granting her the courage to continue. She put the car back on the road, determined to make it back home and secure her family's future, no matter the cost.

❦   4   ❦

Justice pulled into an alley, the headlights of her car casting a shadow on the graffiti-covered walls. Her heart thumped as she killed the engine. Jamal, her younger brother, sat in the passenger seat, his eyes filled with curiosity.

Justice had to stop by their apartment to pick Jamal up. He was blowing up her phone after realizing she hadn't come home. He worried for her, and now that they were together, he wouldn't lose sight of her.

"Stay right here," Justice said. She planned to meet Keisha, deliver the car, and discuss the events in VA.

"Where you going?" Jamal asked.

"Just meeting a friend," she replied with a forced smile, hoping it would ease his concerns. "I won't be long."

Despite the risk, leaving Jamal in the car was her only option. Her father had always taught her to protect her younger brother, and she was going to do just that, even if it meant lying and keeping secrets.

As she stepped out of the car, Justice glanced back at Jamal, who was staring out the window, watching her every move. The weight of her double life was getting heavier as she walked into the darkness of the alley.

Questions burned in Justice's mind as she walked through the door of the meeting spot. The smell of cigarette smoke hung in the air, underscoring the tense atmosphere.

Keisha, seated at a table in the back, eyed Justice's empty hands with a subtle disappointment. There was no warm welcome, no concern for Justice's safety; Keisha's focus was on the absent bags.

"Where's the bags?" Her voice was as cold as ice.

Justice felt her blood boil at the callousness in Keisha's tone. Just hours ago, her life hung by a thread, yet all Keisha cared about were the bags. It stoked the anger inside of her.

Fire ignited in Justice's eyes. Caught in a deceitful trap, she had to uncover the truth. She reached into her waistband and brandished the gun, her emotions a turbulent storm.

"Bitch, you set me up?" She waved the unloaded weapon close to Keisha's face.

The room grew silent with others in the background. The situation had potential for fatality at any moment.

"Set you up? Justice, I have no idea what you're talking about," Keisha stammered. "Put the gun down, please." She begged.

Justice's hand trembled as she held the gun. She couldn't believe Keisha's indifference to the danger she had put her in. "You think it's a joke? People are dead because of you!"

Keisha remained calm, given the circumstances. She took another drag of her cigarette and exhaled. "Justice, sometimes we don't have a choice. Luck made a decision, and we had to follow through. You knew what you signed up for."

"I didn't sign up for murder. I didn't sign up for this shit!"

Keisha's eyes met Justice's. "Listen, sis. I'm sorry you had to go through that. But it's not about what we want. It's about survival, about protecting what's ours."

Justice knew she had to make a decision. She lowered the gun, still keeping a wary eye on Keisha. "I need to know one thing. Are we in this together, or was this all just a setup to get me killed?"

Keisha's expression turned serious. "Justice, you're family, and I would never set you up like that. We're in this together. Now let's figure out how to deal with what's happened."

Justice holstered the gun but didn't trust Keisha. "I'm watching my back from now on. And we need to lay low. This isn't over."

"Luck will take care of that. Don't worry," Keisha assured her, but she also had a burning question she couldn't hold back any longer. "Justice, I need to ask... did you get those bags?"

Justice could no longer contain her fury. She turned around, and as she walked toward the door, she delivered her last words. "Tell Luck to come and get this shit if he wants it..."

In the dead of night, Justice's I-phone rang. She snatched it up, cautious not to disturb her sleeping brother. In a hushed voice, she answered, "Hello?"

"Justice, it's Luck. I'm outside your door," came the voice on the other end.

She shivered when she saw the blocked number on the

screen. Doubt and apprehension tugged at her, but she couldn't ignore the familiarity of his voice. She had to be certain. Pulling the phone away from her ear, she stared at it for a moment before making her move.

With grace, Justice left her bed and approached the front door, her heart beating loudly in the silence of the night. As she peeked through the peephole, she released the breath she was holding when she saw Luck's face on the other side.

"Wassup, you gon' let me in?" His voice was a whisper, but it carried a weight that hinted at the urgency of the moment. Justice hesitated for a second, then unlocked the door and allowed him to step inside.

Luck entered her apartment. The aroma of power and wealth clung to him, and his presence was both comforting and disconcerting. Justice managed a smile as she locked the door behind him.

"Keep your voice down," she cautioned. "My brother's in his room asleep. He has to get up early for school tomorrow."

Luck followed her into the living room, taking a seat beside her on the sofa. He leaned in, his eyes reflecting genuine concern. "First thing I want to say is, under the circumstances, are you okay?"

Justice's heart stirred at his question. Luck had finally asked if she was alright, something she had desperately wanted. She sensed the authenticity in his voice. "I guess," she replied, her emotions a turbulent sea beneath her calm exterior.

"I can only imagine what you had to go through. You sure you okay?" Luck's words dripped with genuine concern, and Justice felt her emotional dam quiver.

Her eyes glistened, and a tear threatened to slip out, but she held it back. "A lil' shaken up by everything that took place. I didn't think I could do something like that," she confided.

Luck leaned back on the sofa, his eyes steady and thoughtful. "In these streets, you find your strength when you're pushed to the edge, and resilience blooms from the cracks in the pavement," he mused. "Something I read in a book a while back."

Justice locked her gaze onto his, her eyes searching for a deeper understanding. "Who were those guys?" she questioned, seeking answers.

Luck's expression darkened as he exhaled. "Some dudes I thought were official. Trust me, I would have never put you in that situation if I would've known they were some foul niggas. That's not how I play," he assured her.

Justice felt the sincerity in Luck's voice, and it brought a sense of reassurance. She believed in him and the bond they had.

"I was afraid I wouldn't make it home to take care of my brother. I don't know if I'm cut out for this lifestyle, Luck."

Luck sat up, his expression sympathetic as he reached out and took Justice's hand. "I'm sorry you had to go through that. I thought it would be an in-and-out thing, which is why I told Keisha to let you handle it," he admitted.

Justice took a deep breath, determined to face the reality of her choices. "I got the money and the drugs," she informed him. "The two duffle bags are in the closet," she said, pointing toward the designated spot. "And the drugs are still in the return car. I didn't want to bring that into my apartment with my little brother here."

Luck nodded, acknowledging her judgment and protective instincts. "You did good, Justice. I promise this won't happen again," he assured her as he stood up. "I'm here for you, and I'm going to make sure you're safe."

Justice retrieved the duffle bags from the closet. "It's all there," she affirmed. "Seven hundred and fifty thousand. Damn, that's a lot of money," she murmured.

Luck took the bags from her, unzipping one of them to reveal the stacks of crisp bills within. He plucked out two stacks, totaling fifty thousand dollars, and extended them toward Justice. His expression was both empathetic and resolute. "That's fifty thousand. I know there's no amount that can ease your discomfort about what took place, but this is a start," he said, his eyes filled with understanding.

He looked around the modest, cramped apartment, recognizing the limitations of her living situation. "You need to get out of this apartment too," he advised. "I got a spot downtown that you and your little brother can crash at. It's nothing spectacular, but it's low key and serves its purpose. Here's the key," he concluded, passing her a key that represented a potential fresh start in a unique environment.

Tears puddled in Justice's eyes as she stood there, holding the stacks of money, and a key to an apartment that represented a new beginning for her and her little brother. She couldn't find the words to express her appreciation, as she was overwhelmed with gratitude. Her father's lessons played back in her mind, reminding her that hard work could lead to a better life, and now she seized it.

"Thank you," she finally said. "You don't have to do this. This is a lot. Are you sure?"

Luck's smile was warm and reassuring as he moved closer to her. His eyes locked onto hers, "Justice, I told you, I got you..."

With a gentle kiss on her forehead, he turned and left her apartment, his presence leaving a mark on her heart.

Jamal breathed hard as he listened to the conversation between his sister and the man known as Luck. He couldn't believe what he was hearing. He noticed his sister's odd behavior, but had no idea she was involved in such matters. Fear and concern took hold of him as he tried to make sense of it all.

In the hallway, he watched, his eyes wide. Being cautious, Jamal concealed his wakefulness and attentiveness to avoid detection. The safety of his sister and their future were at stake; he needed more information. The secrets he was about to uncover would change their lives forever.

Justice collapsed onto the sofa, the weight of the world on her shoulders. She clutched the two stacks of money and the keys to their new apartment, her fingertips trembling as they brushed over the cold, hard cash. A single tear formed in the corner of her eye, clinging to her lash before slipping down her cheek.

The world she had stepped into was demanding, ruthless, and unpredictable, yet it was the only choice she had to secure a future for her and her younger brother. Each passing day, street life squeezed her tighter like a vice.

As she wrestled with her internal chaos, a sudden rustle of footsteps broke the silence, and panic took over. She concealed the money and keys beneath a sofa pillow. Her heart beat skipped as Jamal appeared in her line of sight, his presence unexpected.

"Hey, Jamal," she greeted. Her secret burden and chosen path remained concealed under a deceptive normalcy, yet her life was far from ordinary.

She forced a smile, hoping to reassure her little brother. With a curious expression, Jamal sensed something amiss as he surveyed the room.

"Yeah, I couldn't sleep," he replied, still eyeing the room. He noticed his sister appeared preoccupied and fidgety. His intuition hinted at a deeper narrative.

Justice tried to keep up the façade, but knew she had to divert his attention. "It's just been a long day, you know. But I'm okay," she insisted, all the while praying he would let the matter drop.

Jamal, not convinced but not wanting to press the issue further, nodded and forced a small smile. "Alright, sis. Just remember, I'm here if you ever need to talk."

As he headed back to his room, Justice sighed with relief. Her double life was becoming complex, and the burden of keeping it hidden from her brother was a task in itself. She realized she needed to escape this dangerous world before it consumed her.

LYNCHBURG, VIRGINIA

Federal agents, Robert "Rob" Parker and Samantha "Sam" Wells, moved about the crime scene with a sense of urgency. Their expressions matched the atmosphere that came with the territory.

Rob, a former marine, and a seasoned veteran of the Bureau,

bore a rugged appearance. His close cropped salt-and-pepper beard matched his callous eyes. His reputation was well known among law enforcement circles, marked by his knack for solving the unsolvable and a commitment to seeking justice. Despite his gruff exterior, he was a stickler for detail, always methodical in his approach to cases.

Samantha, an expert in profiling and psychology, and a rising star in the agency, walked with an air of sophistication that often contradicted the gritty nature of their work. A determination to prove herself in a male-dominated field complemented her sharp, analytical mind. Her empathy, an attribute that allowed her to navigate the complexities of criminal investigations with a unique blend of compassion and shrewdness, made her well-known.

Together, these two federal agents were a fierce team, sought after for the most challenging cases that spanned the country. The presence of these two agents at the murder scene in Lynchburg, VA, signaled the gravity of the situation and the scrutiny they would give to dismantling the web of mysteries surrounding the crime.

Rob squatted down to examine the gunshot patterns in the kitchen, his eyes narrowing in concentration. "Sam, someone fired these shots at close range," he informed. "The victims didn't stand a chance."

Samantha, her eyes fixed on the bullet-riddled walls, replied, "Looks like it could've been a hit. There's no sign of struggle here."

Rob nodded. "The real question is, who could have executed this kind of operation? The brutality, the precision... it was well-orchestrated."

As they analyzed the scene, Samantha contemplated the motives. "Drugs, maybe? Gang-related? It could be a turf war."

Rob agreed, but his instincts told him there was more to it. "We can't rule that out, but there's something off about this whole thing, Sam. We need to dig deeper. This feels like a power play, sending a message."

Samantha looked at Rob. "Whoever did this knew what they were doing. It's not a simple hit. It's a statement."

Two agents exchanged a glance, knowing the murder investigation in Lynchburg, VA, would lead them into organized crime and murder.

They combed through the house, documenting evidence, and discussing potential leads. There were bags of cocaine, marijuana, bullet casings, and bloodstains scattered throughout the room, signs of a drug operation gone bad. Yet, something didn't quite fit the scene.

Samantha leaned down to examine a blood-stained wallet on the floor. She picked it up with gloved hands, opening it to reveal a badge and identification. Her eyes widened as she read the badge number, and she turned to Rob with a shocked expression.

"Rob, you're not going to believe this," Samantha said, holding up the badge. "It's a government agent's badge. Special Agent Eric Hayes, DEA."

Rob's eyebrows furrowed as he walked over, looking at the badge. "What's a DEA agent doing here in Lynchburg? This isn't making sense. What was a government agent doing in a house with drug traffickers?" Rob's expression darkened as he tried to make the connection.

Samantha was quick to access their federal database, searching for any recent operations or investigations involving

Agent Hayes. A series of documents popped up, and she clicked on one. The screen displayed an ongoing operation to infiltrate a major drug cartel led by a notorious figure named "Lucian 'Luck' Beckford."

"Rob," Samantha said in a hushed tone, her eyes glued to the screen. "It looks like Agent Hayes was undercover, working to bust a massive drug trafficking ring headed by this guy 'Luck.' The mission was to penetrate the cartel, gather evidence, and make high-profile arrests."

Rob's mind raced, his thoughts swirling with implications. "This was supposed to be a secret operation. They went in deep-cover, and something must have gone wrong."

Samantha nodded. "Maybe Luck's organization got wind of their true identities and retaliated? But it's not just about their safety now; if Luck discovers their connection to the DEA, it could compromise our entire operation."

The discovery sent shockwaves through the investigation. Justice's involvement in this case had her trapped in a web of danger far greater than she had ever imagined. Answers were just starting to be sought, and the stakes had intensified.

The Cathedral of St. Michael in Manhattan stood tall, its sacred halls bearing witness to the alliance that was forming within. As the sunlight filtered through the stained glass windows, painting colorful patterns on the marble floor, the atmosphere inside was thick with hostility and greed.

A long, ornate table was headed by Luck. Seated across from him, the notorious leader of one of the most feared Mexican drug cartels was a man known as El Cazador. His real name,

Pedro Ramirez. He was a burly man with a grim visage, his features hardened by a life of ruthless decision-making and a trail of violence.

El Cazador, which meant "The Hunter" in Spanish, had earned his nickname for his pursuit of power and control in the drug trade. The Ramirez cartel was infamous for its cunning tactics, merciless enforcement, and elaborate network of operatives.

Dressed in a sharp black suit, El Cazador engaged in the high-stakes negotiation with Luck. His presence alone commanded respect and fear, making it clear that the cartel leader was not a man to be fucked with.

"Senor," El Cazador said with a heavy accent, "I have given you enough for this operation. Kidnapping a high political figure is no small feat."

Luck leaned forward. "You and I both know that the stakes are higher than ever. This ain't just any politician; it's a fuckin' senator. We need more money to pull this off."

El Cazador's eyes narrowed, and he leaned back in his chair. "I've already committed substantial resources to this. My people are in place, and the plan is in motion."

"Then we better make sure nothing goes wrong. And that means getting those extra funds I need."

As they continued their negotiation, Luck's crew, each one a hardened criminal from various backgrounds, filled the cathedral's pews. The cathedral's sacred space served as a backdrop to their nefarious plotting.

Bishop William Ryan, a man of the cloth, delivered a sermon on the sacredness of life and the commandment against murder at the altar. His words vibrated through the cathedral, creating a disconcerting contrast between his sermon and the dark dealings at the table.

"Thou shalt not kill," he said, raising his voice as if to punctuate the commandment. "For life is a gift from the Almighty, and it is not for us to take."

In the cramped apartment at the Jacob Riis housing projects, Justice sat on the frayed couch. Her expression held the weight of her secrets. She found it exhausting to hide her dangerous double life from Jamal. Each lie she told him chipped away at her conscience.

She observed Jamal, transformed into a young man, tending to his responsibilities, displaying the same strength she had always shown for him. But he couldn't help but notice the changes in his sister's demeanor, the late nights she spent away from home, and the whispered conversations that never seemed to have a rational explanation.

That night, he couldn't forget hearing her talk in the living room. It was the night everything unraveled, and he knew he couldn't ignore his growing suspicion any longer. He could sense the distance that had grown between them and the burden that weighed on Justice's shoulders.

As the days went by, Jamal wrestled with his desire to trust his sister and his gut feeling that something was different. He couldn't bear the thought of facing the truth, but he also couldn't let her spiral into a world of secrets and danger without questioning her choices. Their bond was at stake, and he knew that soon he would have to confront her and uncover the secrets that threatened to tear them apart.

As Justice sat on the worn sofa, her fingers traced the edges of the key that symbolized a new beginning in their lives. It had been a month since Luck had handed her the key, and she'd spent that time thinking about how to break the news to Jamal.

The lie about her new, high-paying job lingered. It was the seed for her apartment story. She knew Jamal wasn't a child anymore; he was smart and intuitive. The more she lied, the closer he came to discovering the truth.

Justice had always been protective of her little brother, shielding him from the world. Holding the key, she knew it was time to reveal their future. With a deep breath, she readied herself for the conversation that lay ahead, acknowledging that they were about to write the next chapter in their book of life.

❦   5   ❦

In their new Tribeca loft, Justice couldn't help but feel a sense of relief and gratitude as she settled into a better life for her and Jamal. The loft, with its ample light and large windows, felt like a world apart from the cramped apartment in the Jacob Riis housing projects. The upgrade was thanks to Luck, the man who showed her a new life.

However, as the days passed, Jamal's curiosity grew, and Justice couldn't ignore the probing questions he had asked. Being an inquisitive younger brother, every question felt like deception to Justice.

Jamal's questions came, each one fueling his fascination with his sister's supposed new job. He was interested in knowing about her company, coworkers, and work. Each question, though innocent in his eyes, was a test of Justice's ability to weave a convincing tale.

Justice did her best to maintain her composure, keeping up her facade of a legitimate job, but she could sense the web of lies becoming a tangled mess. Creating new falsehoods daily, aligning them with the old ones, was an ordeal. Each fabrication was a potential minefield, and keeping them consistent was, in itself, a full-time job.

Their conversations often played out in the loft's open space, with Jamal's curiosity driving him to ask more questions, and Justice struggling to maintain her constructed reality. The tension in their back-and-forth conversations heightened as Jamal's innocent curiosity posed a threat to exposing the truth that Justice was desperate to protect.

This constant need for deception was heavy, and Justice couldn't help but worry about what might happen when the lies she told begin to crumble under the weight of her brother's inquisitiveness.

The loft was an upgrade from their previous living conditions, but it was feeling like a pressure cooker for Justice and Jamal. On this day, the tension between them reached its boiling point.

Jamal had been doing some research about the area they now lived in, and he couldn't believe what he had discovered about the astronomical rent prices. The concern had been building inside him, and he could no longer keep it to himself.

"Justice, we need to talk," he said.

Justice looked up from her book, her face painted with innocence. "Sure, what's up?"

Jamal held up a piece of paper he had found during his research. "What's this? Some kind of joke?"

Justice took the paper and her heart sank. It was a rental notice, showing the monthly cost of their loft, and the amount was staggering. She hoped Jamal wouldn't find out, but her brother was too smart for that.

"Jamal, it's not what you think," she said.

But Jamal didn't stop. He stormed over to a closet and flung open the door. Inside, he found a black box, and inside that box, the weight of the truth. The gun she had used back in Lynchburg, Virginia, lay there, wrapped in a t-shirt, harmless and empty of bullets.

"What's this?" Jamal's voice quivered with anger.

Justice struggled to find the right words, and she could see that her brother's trust in her was eroding.

"Jamal, there's a lot you don't know, things I can't explain," she began, her eyes filling with tears.

But Jamal wasn't having it. "You can't keep lying to me, Justice. Not anymore. I'm scared, and I need to understand what's going on."

The argument escalated from there, voices raised and emotions running high. Jamal's fear and confusion mixed with Justice's own frustration at the impossible situation she had gotten them into.

Their heated conversation was loud throughout the loft. It was a reminder that their bond was being strained to its limits by the secrets and danger that had become a part of their lives.

A few days later, Keisha sent Justice a text message to let her know she would be stopping by, and she'd have Bishop and Ox with her. An hour later, Justice opened the door to welcome Keisha, Bishop, and Ox. The moment intensified as they entered the loft, thickening the air. The low hum of the city outside was the only background noise. Keisha's arrival carried an aura of apprehension and lingering mistrust.

"Hey," Justice said with a forced smile as she welcomed them in. Her experiences had made her cautious, especially around Keisha. She couldn't forget what had transpired in

Lynchburg, but the business demanded some level of cooperation.

With a nod, Keisha moved further into the loft, flanked by Bishop and Ox. They were younger, street-hardened guys, and it showed in their demeanor. Their eyes were sharp, scanning the room.

As the group settled in, Justice offered them seating, gesturing to the couch and a couple of chairs. It was a mismatched assortment of furniture in their spacious loft. Each piece had its own story, and it felt symbolic of the disjointed lives they were living.

"Let's get down to business," Keisha said, her tone serious. The clinking of gold jewelry on her wrists was an unsettling contrast to the atmosphere. "Luck needs these boys to move more product, and he wants you to be their point person."

The words "point person" rang in Justice's ears like an alarm. She was becoming further entrenched in this dangerous world, a responsibility she couldn't shirk.

Bishop and Ox sat on the edge of the couch and exchanged glances. Justice held the reins on their drug distribution efforts, and they knew it. Their loyalty was tied to her decision.

Darren Lindsey, better known as Bishop, and Orlando Brown, dubbed Ox, were two young men who were climbing the ranks of the drug trade, bringing a volatile mix of swag and recklessness to the streets.

Justice accepted the proposal. While discussing details, Jamal entered, and the atmosphere changed. His presence disrupted the conversations, and everyone turned their attention toward him. Justice knew that their facade of a stable, ordinary life was slipping through her fingers.

Jamal scanned the room, his eyes shifting from one face to

another. Keisha, who had been a looming presence in their lives, exuded an air of authority that wasn't lost on him. Bishop, the older of the two newcomers, had a confident but scrutinizing look, while Ox's intense and cocky demeanor seemed to create an electric charge in the air.

For a moment, it was silent, and Jamal was the unwitting intruder.

Justice sprang to her feet, her eyes darting to her brother. He stood there in the doorway, baffled by the unfamiliar faces in their living room. "Hey, Jamal," she said, her voice tinged with nervousness. "Everything alright?"

Jamal's eyes fixed on Keisha, who he recognized as Justice's friend. He then turned his attention to the two strangers, Bishop and Ox. Their presence set off alarm bells in his mind. "Who are these people?" Jamal questioned, a hint of concern in his voice.

Justice gestured to each of them, her expression tense. "Well, you know my friend Keisha. And that's Bishop and Ox."

Ox leaned forward, offering a casual greeting. "What's good, homie?"

For a moment, Jamal locked eyes with Bishop, the name stirring a sense of déjà vu within him. But without a clear memory, he turned on his heels and retreated to his room, leaving the group to their conversation.

Keisha laughed, her eyes on the closed door. "What was that about?"

Justice, still aware of how nosy her brother could be, managed a smirk. "You know Jamal, he's very protective of his sister."

With Jamal's concerns brushed aside, they continued their discussion on the operation. It became clear that Justice would be the point person for drug distribution, working with Bishop and Ox, who would report to her when they needed more product. They would take care of street-level transactions with their network of dealers.

As the plans unfolded, it struck Justice that all the money flowing through Bishop and Ox would pass through her hands before reaching Luck. She couldn't quite understand why Luck had so much trust in her.

Jamal scrolled through his Instagram feed, tapping the 'like' button on photos that caught his attention. He lost himself in the online world, swiping past various posts of people flexing their lives on the platform. But then, it happened. There he was, in all his flamboyant glory: Bishop.

Jamal stared at the image of Bishop, sitting in a shiny red Ferrari. In his hand, a jaw-dropping stack of money flaunting it like a rapper's prop. The backdrop was the heart of New York City, with skyscrapers in the background. Bishop's swag was undeniable, as was his online clout.

Jamal knew he recognized the face. He was that dude who hung out with the young, up-and-coming New York rappers. On Instagram, Bishop's account boasted over one hundred thousand followers. The drill rap scene, a thriving subculture in the city, was all the rage among these artists, and Jamal had found himself immersed in the genre.

It was more than just music; it was a lifestyle. And as Jamal studied Bishop's pictures and posts, he couldn't help but wonder how his sister had become connected to this world. The boundaries between their lives were blurring, and the allure of the streets tugged at Jamal's curiosity like a magnetic force.

On a sunny Sunday morning, Justice couldn't contain her excitement. With a birthday cake in her hands, she tiptoed into Jamal's room, hoping to surprise him. As she reached his bedside, she couldn't hold it in any longer.

"Happy Birthday!" she exclaimed, her voice filled with joy as she thrust the cake toward her brother.

Startled from sleep, Jamal's eyes popped open, and he blinked away the crust that clung to the corners. He squinted at the cake and the envelope she held out to him, realizing the occasion.

"Thanks, sis..." he mumbled, his voice still thick with sleep. He reached out to accept the envelope, eager to know what might be inside.

With a grin, Justice awaited his response. "What you wanna do today?" she asked.

Jamal rubbed his eyes and tried to gauge the time. The numbers on the alarm clock confirmed his early-morning suspicion.

"Justice, it's seven in the morning," he chuckled, his sleepy laughter punctuating his words. "Go away."

Justice couldn't help but laugh, too. It was Jamal's 17th birthday, and she was determined to make it memorable, even if he preferred a little more sleep.

Jamal forced himself out of bed, trying to shake off the drowsiness. A refreshing shower, followed by a quick selection of clothes for the day, helped rouse him from the remnants of sleep.

When Jamal walked towards the dining room, he was greeted by an unexpected and delightful sight. The kitchen table displayed a sumptuous breakfast spread, giving the impression that it belonged in a five-star restaurant. There was browned French toast, plump beef sausages, crispy beef bacon, creamy grits, and fluffy scrambled eggs. The dishes filled the room with a mouth-watering aroma.

"Damn, sis..." Jamal exclaimed, pulling out a chair to sit at the table. "You did your thing, huh?"

Justice beamed with pride. The joy of celebrating her brother's special day was clear in her eyes. "A lil' something for my bro," she said, her smile growing wider. "Happy Birthday again, Jamal. I love you." She leaned in and gave him a warm hug, expressing the deep affection she held for her younger brother.

At the kitchen table, the two siblings savored the breakfast before them, basking in the simple pleasure of each other's company. It had been a while since they had shared a meal and a genuine conversation, a tradition they had maintained with their late father. They talked, laughed, and shared memories of their dad, shedding tears as they released pent-up emotions.

The heartfelt moment meant everything to them. Justice had been pulled into a life of crime and responsibility, leaving little room for being present in her brother's life. However, sitting there with Jamal, she could just be a regular sister, and it was a welcomed break from the constant turmoil of their current reality.

As they enjoyed the breakfast and shared stories, Justice's thoughts wandered towards the future. She realized her current life was not viable for the future. The criminal world was dangerous, and she needed an escape plan. It was a moment of calm, but it allowed her to reflect on her journey and contemplate what lay ahead.

As the day progressed, Justice and Jamal embarked on a lavish shopping spree, and Justice spared no expense to indulge her little brother's every wish. She was determined to make his 17th birthday an unforgettable one, showering him with gifts and allowing him to select anything his heart desired.

As they drove in her Mercedes Benz, their favorite tunes blaring from the speakers, Jamal reached for the volume control and lowered the music. Justice was taken aback and protested, "What are you doing? That's my jam!"

Jamal, however, appeared serious and determined, a complete difference from the jovial mood that had filled the car moments before. "Hold up, sis," he said, turning his gaze towards the road as they sped down the highway. "This is important. I need some answers."

Justice sensed the gravity of the situation as Jamal's tone grew more somber. "What's on your mind, little bro?" she asked, with a deep breath to steady herself. The questions had her at a crossroads. She could either continue weaving the web of lies she had spun or face the truth and reveal her secrets.

"How you know, Bishop?" he asked.

The question lingered momentarily. She decided it was time to reveal at least a part of the truth to her brother.

Taking her eyes off the road for a moment, she looked at Jamal and replied, "Bishop... he's connected to some people I met through my job."

The words fell from her lips, and she could see the confusion and concern in Jamal's eyes.

Back at the loft, as Justice was immersed in her room,

analyzing numbers and negotiating drug deals, she couldn't help but feel the pressure of her responsibilities. The lead distributor role was demanding constant attention and swift decision-making. Trapped in an unwanted life, she felt stuck in a never-ending cycle.

Meanwhile, Jamal, in the living room, had his senses consumed by the beats and lyrics of the latest drill rap music videos. The volume was maxed out as he rapped gritty verses, each line depicting street reality. The music offered him a momentary escape from the confusion surrounding his sister's actions.

As Justice emerged from her room, the intense, raw energy of the music blaring from the television struck her. She tried to engage with Jamal. "What is this, Jamal?" she asked. However, Jamal was so caught up in the music that her presence went unnoticed.

Growing more irritated with his detachment, Justice raised her voice. "Jamal!" she shouted, but her words seemed to be swallowed by the beat. Frustration took hold, and she took matters into her own hands. She moved forward and grabbed the remote from the table. With a press of the mute button, the room fell into silence.

Startled, Jamal turned around, his eyes wide with disbelief at the sudden silence. "What happened? I was listening to that," he said, bewildered by his sister's interference.

Justice couldn't hide her disdain as she scrunched up her face, looking at the television screen. "What is this mess, Jamal?"

Jamal was enthusiastic about the song that had swept through the city. He answered his sister, "That's G-Wokaz's new hit, 'Spin The Block.'"

Justice shook her head, unimpressed. "It sounds terrible. And they're not saying anything substantial. All they rap about is killing each other. Since when did you start listening to this kind of music?"

"C'mon, Justice," he responded, a hint of defensiveness in his voice. "It's the new hot song. Everybody's on it. Look," he urged, pointing at the screen. "Your friend Bishop is in this video."

Justice glanced at the TV and saw Bishop in the music video, waving a gun and displaying money on a table. Her eyes widened as she took in the sight. She hadn't known about Bishop's involvement in the entertainment industry, and seeing him in a video that glorified guns and money was unsettling. It was a poor reflection on their drug business. It was a risk that threatened their underground dealings.

Justice inhaled deep, struggling to contain her concerns, but she couldn't ignore the gravity of the situation. Her mind raced, contemplating the implications of Bishop's actions and the potential impact on their already complex lives.

In an era where information flows at the tap of a screen, social media held both a captivating allure and a delicate edge. Jamal, raised in the digital age, experienced life as a stream of images and videos, memories flickering with a swipe.

Lately, Jamal had become entrenched in the social media universe. Alongside his friends, they captured every moment, no matter how ordinary or extraordinary, and shared it with the world. The air was thick with a sense of urgency to live up to the streetwise persona they presented. Their generation was defined by a desire to emulate the tough lifestyle glorified in their posts and rap lyrics.

In this digital metaverse, reality intertwined with fiction, and ordinary individuals became digital heroes, warriors of their own stories. The internet had amplified voices that once went unheard, turning everyday people into experts and influencers, holding the answers to life's questions.

In the streets of Harlem, Jamal had found a new circle of friends, schoolmates whose mischievous adventures held an undeniable allure. Their adolescent hearts beat in harmony with a shared quest for mischief, daring the world to put up a fight. As Jamal hung around with this rowdy bunch, the pressures of peer influence grew with every passing day.

Trying hard to blend in, Jamal struggled to maintain the front that masked his true self. Beneath it all, he possessed a moral compass that clashed with his new friends' ways. Jamal's innocence was at odds with his environment, and the pull of peer pressure tugged at the edges of his conscience.

In the pursuit to fit in, Jamal felt a burning need to prove himself, to showcase his allegiance to his so-called friends. He was unaware that the comrades he sought approval from were not true friends. The path he was on held many hidden twists, revealing the complexities of youthful influence and a young man's longing for acceptance.

Alone in the loft one day, Jamal found himself flushed with boredom. To fend off the restlessness, he sifted through the hallway closet. His search was aimless, a casual exploration of the forgotten nooks and crannies of his surroundings. However, amid the disarray of forgotten items, his fingers brushed against a black box. He remembered what was in the box. Surprised that Justice hadn't removed it, he opened it to reveal the empty firearm wrapped in an old, tattered t-shirt.

Jamal had never held a gun, and feeling it in his hands carried an electrifying sense of power. As he cradled it with caution, he couldn't help but contemplate the rush that came with it.

A thought, both sinister and exhilarating, went through Jamal's mind—*what if he were to have this power?* Holding the gun, he adopted an intimidating demeanor, even while alone in that closet. His reflection in the iPhone camera lens became his audience as he snapped pictures and shared them across his social media profiles.

With each snapshot, Jamal felt a satisfaction, a sense of accomplishment for having dared to tamper with forces beyond his grasp. Little did he know that the source of his momentary triumph might soon become a harbinger of unforeseen consequences, a turning point in his life filled with both laughter and tears.

Late on a Friday night, anxiety gnawed at Justice's nerves as she paced the living room, her fingers wrapped around a glass of wine. The clock had already ticked past 1 am, and Jamal hadn't returned home yet. Panic built as she had attempted to call his phone and sent a flurry of unanswered text messages. Terrifying scenarios filled her mind as she let her imagination run wild, thinking of where he could be caught up. *What if something had happened to Jamal?* The thought bothered her with increasing urgency.

Just as her anxiety was spiraling into panic, her phone sprung to life with an unknown number. Without a moment's hesitation, she snatched it up. "Hello?" she answered.

Heavy silence filled the line, followed by a familiar voice. "It's me, sis... Jamal," he said.

"Jamal, where are you?"

"I'm at the seventeenth precinct. I got arrested."

Justice felt the world dissolve as the word "arrested" lingered in her mind. Panic and dread bubbled inside of her. "Arrested? For what, Jamal?"

"I had some Za," he admitted.

"Za? What the hell is that?"

"It's weed, Justice. The cops arrested me and my friend for smoking."

"Weed?" Justice's eyes got wide. "What are you doing smoking weed, Jamal? What's going on?" The situation felt surreal to her. As far as she knew, Jamal hadn't shown any inclination toward drug use or any activities that could land him in jail. It just made little sense.

"Sis, I just need you to come down here and get me. They told me I have to see a judge and get bail," Jamal informed her, his voice tinged with desperation.

As her brother's words washed over her, Justice knew she had to act quick, despite the whirlwind of confusion she felt. She needed to get Jamal out of this dilemma.

Jamal watched as the judge banged the gavel and handed down a bail of $1,000. He knew he had let his sister down.

Justice bailed him out, but the ride home was anything but calm. Tension filled the air, choking any attempts at conversation. The silence was thick as both siblings grappled with their emotions.

Justice's mind was a chaotic battleground of insane thoughts. She felt a mix of disappointment, heartbreak, and frustration. The sting was overshadowed by guilt. She couldn't help but wonder if the choices she had made, the path she was on, had cast an inescapable shadow on Jamal's life.

As her grip on the steering wheel tightened, Justice fought to hold back a flood of tears, her emotions a sea of regret and self-reproach. She wished she could scream, to vent the frustration and turmoil that had enveloped her. But she knew it wouldn't change the reality they both faced.

As they entered the loft, the tension was heavy. Justice knew it was time to address the underlying issue, to confront her brother about the choices he was making. With a deep breath, she broke the silence.

"What happened to your dreams, Jamal?" she asked, concerned and sad at the same time. Jamal had once harbored aspirations of becoming a Gold Medal Olympic swimmer, and he was passionate about helping others achieve their dreams as well. His father had taught him the value of being positive. However, his current path seemed to distance him from his goals.

Jamal's eyes met his sister's, and his response was raw and drenched in pain. "My dreams died when Dad passed," he told her, his voice heavy with the weight of that loss. "What do you want me to do, Justice?"

The room seemed to close in on them as they struggled with the emotions swirling between them. Jamal's question was a plea for understanding and guidance, but it was also a reminder of the choices they both had to make.

Justice, being the older sister, had always protected. She saw herself as the one responsible for Jamal's future and wellbeing, guiding him away from the dangers of the street. Yet, she couldn't deny that her involvement in Luck's organization was having an influence on her brother. His brush with the law over marijuana had shaken her to her core.

Jamal felt the peer pressure and the glamour of the streets. He was in a fragile place, searching for a sense of identity and belonging after losing their father. His dreams of becoming an Olympic swimmer had faded, replaced by a growing immersion in the street culture. He, too, was struggling with his role in their strained relationship.

The loft that they once called home felt like a war zone of silent tension, unspoken questions, and misunderstandings. Justice wrestled with her own guilt, questioning whether her choices were the root of Jamal's downward spiral. Jamal sought a way to reconcile the person he was becoming with the dreams he had once held dear.

Their relationship had reached a crossroads, and both were standing on the edge of tough decisions. The strains that pulled them apart were threatening to snap, and the path forward was uncertain. The days and weeks ahead will determine if the family's bonds can withstand the choices they made.

$$\text{❧} \quad 6 \quad \text{❧}$$

In the office at the heart of the FBI headquarters, Agents Parker and Wells were wrestling with frustration. The murder of DEA agent Eric Hayes, a year gone cold, had become an enigma. The case board loomed before them: images, notes, and unanswered questions. It was evidence of their efforts, which had produced little.

Parker leaned forward, eyes locked on the board, as if the pictures themselves held the missing pieces of the puzzle. Among the clutter of information, there were only two photographs that seemed to matter: the picture of Lucian "Luck" Beckford and, of particular interest now, his sister Keisha Beckford.

Agent Wells, determined to make progress, leaned in, breaking the silence with a suggestion. "What about the sister? Maybe it'll be easier to get to her. We get her on something good, and maybe she'll cooperate."

Parker considered the idea, a smile tugging at the corner of his lips. It was the plan that could crack the case. With a deliberate motion, he pulled Keisha's photo from the board and stared at it. "In this game, you don't hunt the lions first; you start by trapping the alley cats. They'll lead you to the kings..."

In the spacious, joy-filled dining hall, pink and blue balloons swayed in the air, adding to the atmosphere of celebration. Keisha, seated like a queen on her throne, was the radiant center of attention. Her wide smile lit up the room, and her belly pronounced at 7.5 months pregnant. Friends and family had gathered to shower her with love and gifts, marking the occasion with laughter, chatter, and the rustling of wrapping paper.

When the invitation to Keisha's baby shower had arrived in the mail, it took Justice by surprise. She had sensed a growing distance between them, but the news of Keisha's pregnancy filled her with both joy and complicated emotions. Despite the feelings that tugged at her heart, she had accepted the invite, choosing to celebrate with Keisha in a room filled with warmth.

The festivities continued, and Justice immersed herself in the happiness. She danced, laughed, sipped on her drink, and engaged in the surrounding conversations. At one point, she found herself reflecting on her own life journey and the choices that had brought her to this point.

During the excited atmosphere of Keisha's baby shower, Justice's eyes remained fixed on her friend as she unwrapped her gifts. A pang of nostalgia took her back to her mother, who left when Justice was seven. Her memories were scarce, and her younger brother, Jamal, only three, hadn't known her at all.

As Keisha revealed each present, Justice couldn't help but wonder what her mother would have been like. There was only one photograph of her that Justice held close, and it was the words of their father that connected her image to the memories she wished she had. Justice, with her father's strength and features, often wondered whether she resembled her mother in spirit and appearance.

Her thoughts shifted to their father, the cornerstone of their lives. He had dedicated himself to provide for his children, working long hours day and night. More than a provider, he was a mentor, instilling life lessons that would remain in Justice's memory forever, shaping her into the strong woman she had become.

Keisha approached Justice, who was seated. A smile of appreciation graced her lips. "Thank you for coming, Justice," Keisha said, her voice filled with genuine gratitude.

Justice rose from her seat, her eyes drawn to Keisha's burgeoning belly. "Girl, your belly is huge," she exclaimed with a chuckle, offering Keisha a warm hug. They embraced, sharing a moment of joy and camaraderie. The room echoed with laughter, reflecting the joy of the occasion.

Taking in the surroundings, Justice couldn't help but compliment her friend. "This is beautiful, Keisha. Congratulations on everything."

Keisha's eyes filled up with emotion, and she reached out to touch Justice's arm. "Thank you, Justice. I know we've had some issues, but you've always been a loyal friend to me, and I respect you for that," Keisha confided, her voice filled with sincerity and warmth.

The noise and celebration of the baby shower receded into the background as the two friends engaged in a heartfelt conversation. In that moment, it was just Keisha and Justice, sharing their thoughts and feelings with an intimacy that transcended the room's ambiance.

In a shift of conversation, Keisha leaned in closer, her voice lowered to ensure their words remained between them. "Has Luck spoken to you about Ox?" she asked with a concerned tone, her eyes fixed on Justice. The week had passed with no word from Luck, and Justice's sense of unease was growing.

"I haven't talked to Luck," Justice responded. She hoped to see him at the baby shower, but he wasn't there. Her brow furrowed as she continued, "I was hoping I would run into him here."

Keisha nodded, acknowledging the challenging situation Luck was in. "Luck had some other business he had to handle today," she disclosed, choosing her words carefully. However, her focus shifted to the current matter. "As for Ox, he's become a problem, Justice. He's a thief, and he has to be dealt with. Since he's part of your crew, it's up to you to handle it."

Keisha's tone was resolute, emphasizing the urgency of the situation. Justice could feel the weight of the responsibility that came with her position in Luck's organization. As she absorbed the gravity of Keisha's words, she knew that confronting Ox was a challenge she could not avoid.

Justice's fall into the criminal world was never a choice she sought or a path she embarked upon. It was a harrowing journey, one that began with the tragic loss of their father, leaving her with the sole responsibility of caring for herself and her younger brother, Jamal.

After her father's death, the world felt desolate and opportunities for a better life were scarce. The reality threw Justice into a situation where survival held more importance than mere existence.

The criminal world emerged as a lifeline, providing quick cash and a means of survival. Justice wrestled with the moral implications of her choices, but the hunger in her belly was a reminder that faced with adversity, she could ill afford to be picky about the paths she took.

It was a tale of necessity, of the hunger pangs that threatened to consume her and her brother. Justice viewed her criminal involvement as a means to secure life's necessities.

The world Justice had entered was one where the most virtuous heart could wither and transform into something darker, more sinister. Many saw compassion as weakness, disregarding kindness.

Justice's walk had taken her far from the warm and compassionate person she once was. Her heart, once so full of empathy and goodwill, was now encased in a chilling icebox of venom. The toll of her responsibilities was visible in her transformation.

Once warm and radiant, her trademark smile now reflects seriousness. She had adopted a mask of icy determination, an armor necessary for the role she had assumed. In her role as lead distributor for Luck's organization, sentiment and hesitation were irrelevant.

"In these streets," Justice reflected, *"some play the chessboard of life, positioning others as pawns in their game of power. But every pawn has the potential to become a queen."* She replayed the words Luck had once said to her. The message seemed hidden in plain sight, waiting for her to grasp its significance.

Justice's expression shifted from doubt to determination. Her role in this complex world was undeniable, and she knew she couldn't be a pawn in someone else's game. As her realization settled, she understood she was a boss. And a boss made boss moves.

With this fresh energy, she formulated her strategy, determined to handle the Ox situation. Justice had her own power in this game, and she was ready to make her mark.

The sleek Mercedes-Benz pulled to the curb on Halsey Avenue, a shiny embodiment of luxury amidst the rugged concrete landscape. Its impeccable $80,000 paint job sparkled in the morning sun, casting reflections that seemed to dance across its polished surface. The tinted windows, as black as a moonless night, acted as a shield, veiling the car's occupants from prying eyes.

Justice shifted the gear into 'Park' and reached for her phone, her actions precise and calculated. With a determined voice, she uttered, "Call Bishop," and the device dialed the number. Bishop's voice came through the speaker, and Justice got straight to the point.

"I'm out front," she informed him before hanging up.

On the block, a pack of young boys conducted their business, weaving through the chaos with frenzied exchanges. The street came alive, a volatile theater where lives danced with danger.

Curious onlookers approached the car, their curiosity piqued, but the obsidian windows were impenetrable. Whoever was in that car was beyond their reach, and they were well aware of the unspoken rule that Justice was off-limits.

She sat poised in the driver's seat. As she waited for Bishop, she was aware of the silent dance of power taking place all around her. It was a dangerous game, and she was about to make a significant move.

Justice knew the gravity of her next play. Giving a greenlight for a hit wasn't a decision to be taken lightly. With a calm and calculated demeanor, she popped open the glove compartment and retrieved the shiny nine-millimeter, its metallic surface glowing under the sunlight. She stared at it for a moment before cocking the weapon and placing it on her lap.

Minutes later, Bishop emerged from the adjacent building, strutting toward the sleek Mercedes-Benz. He opened the passenger door, and his eyes locked onto the cold steel in Justice's lap. "Wassup, Justice, you good?"

Justice didn't move her eyes from the weapon, a nod serving as an acknowledgment of his question. After a heavy silence, she spoke. "I need you to handle something for me."

"Yeah, whatever you need. I got you."

Justice turned to face him, her eyes burning into his soul. "It's Ox," she said, "he's been stealing. He gotta go."

Bishop attempted to smile. His efforts to downplay the severity of the situation fell flat. But he couldn't ignore the seriousness on her face. His eyes dipped to the gun resting in her lap. "Nah, you for real?" he questioned, though he already knew the answer. "C'mon, Justice... Ox?"

Justice inhaled deep, staring at Bishop. Her hand rested on the firearm. "Listen," she began. "I didn't come here to go back and forth about why or what happened or none of that. I came here to ask you to do something. Are you gonna do it or not?"

Bishop recognized that there was no room for debate as the decision had already been made, and refusing it would have dire consequences. "I got you. Don't worry about it."

Before he exited the car, a last question hung in the air. "What you was gon' do if I said no?"

With a straight face, Justice replied, "Kill you. Now get the fuck outta my car."

Bishop watched as the Mercedes disappeared into the distance. His life depended on carrying out this hit, and it meant taking the life of someone he considered a best friend. Ox wasn't just a friend; they had grown up together, shared countless memories, and played together as kids. They had a deep bond between them, and now it had been tainted.

As Bishop contemplated his decision, he couldn't help but think about Ox's two little girls. They were innocent, and they would grow up without a father, forever affected by the streets that had claimed their dad. A single tear filled Bishop's right eye. He dismissed it, aware that now was not the time for emotions. They had already made the decision, knowing that the code of the streets was ruthless. A green light was on Ox's head, and Bishop was now the appointed executioner.

The Mercedes eased into the secluded parking space behind her building, and Justice shifted the gear into park. As she stared at the passenger seat, her eyes fell on the cold steel gun. It sat there, a silent reason for the transformation she was undergoing. She didn't comprehend what was happening to her, it was beyond her control. The darkness had crept into her soul, suffocating her, and she felt powerless to resist it.

Justice couldn't fight the tide of her own transformation. Her ethical boundaries were now blurred beyond recognition. She transformed into an unexpected version of herself, one who dealt with life and death without hesitation or remorse.

She looked up at the rearview mirror. As she stared at herself, the tears built up and streamed down her face like an unending river. She was a stranger to herself, trapped in a dangerous world she never imagined. She wondered if there was a way out of her self-made hell.

Keisha held up a tiny outfit, her eyes shining with excitement. "This is just the cutest thing ever," she said, showing her friend Kim the adorable baby clothes they'd found in the infant section of Walmart. Keisha had learned the gender of her baby, and the news that she was having a girl filled her with excitement. As they dissected the aisles of baby clothing, neither of them knew that they had been under surveillance for the past hour.

Agent Parker and Agent Wells maintained a careful distance, making sure not to get too close to their subjects as they followed Keisha and her friend. The opportunity to approach Keisha had arrived, and it was crucial for them to seize this chance to gather information.

Keisha and Kim exchanged a quick glance, their unease growing as the two strangers initiated contact. "Ooh, that's a nice one..." Agent Wells commented, trying to engage Keisha in conversation.

Both Keisha and Kim sensed these people were somehow connected to law enforcement. Their standoffish attitude became more apparent, and Keisha rolled her eyes, returning her focus to the clothes they were browsing.

However, the agents were persistent. "Miss Beckford, we need to talk," Agent Parker stated with a sense of urgency.

Keisha turned around. "Do I know you?" she questioned, her eyes locked on the agents.

"I'm federal agent Rob Parker, and this is agent Samantha Wells."

"Federal agent? What you need to talk to me about?"

"It's about your brother, Lucian," agent Parker revealed.

Keisha's heart sank, and she took a deep breath, glancing at her friend Kim, who wore a concerned expression. She then turned her attention back to the agent. "I have nothing to say," she replied with a firm tone, her eyes reflecting her reluctance.

Agent Wells interjected, adopting a more empathetic approach. "We just want to ask you a few questions, Miss Beckford."

But Keisha remained resistant. She sighed heavily and rolled her eyes. "I told you I don't have nothing to say," she emphasized, her eyes darting between Kim and the persistent agents. "Now, can I shop in peace, please?"

Sensing the growing tension in Keisha's voice and her clear reluctance, the two agents eased off. "Alright, Miss Beckford. We don't want to stress you out. Maybe it's the wrong time," Agent Wells suggested, casting a quick glance between Keisha and her friend Kim. "C'mon, Parker. Let's leave these ladies to do their shopping..."

As the two agents walked away, they could hear Keisha and her friend whispering something in the distance, but their words were too soft to discern. Agent Parker turned to Agent Wells. "Did you see what I saw, Wells?" he inquired.

Agent Wells couldn't hide a sly smile. "Yep..."

The encounter with Keisha hadn't unfolded as expected, but both agents sensed she might be willing to talk under different circumstances, away from the watchful eyes of her friend. This new lead was promising, and they understood Keisha might have information that could bring them closer to solving the case.

Jamal focused on the screen, engrossed in his video game, as he fought virtual foes at the loft. The persistent vibrations in his pocket drew his focus away. Frustration building, he ripped off his headset, letting it fall onto the floor with a thud.

He pulled out his phone, noticing three text messages from Bishop. The messages were brief but cryptic.

'Yo, whaddup?'

'You tryna roll out?'

'I'm downstairs. bring that thang wit' you. I got somethin' for you.'

The urgency in Bishop's texts made Jamal excited. He couldn't ignore the sense of mystery and importance in those messages. He typed a response:

'Give me a sec. I'm coming down.'

Deep in his thoughts, Jamal knew exactly what Bishop was texting about. They had discussed it beforehand, and Jamal had agreed to take care of it for him.

Bishop and Jamal had grown close over the past few weeks, their secret bond deepening under the radar of Justice. It all started when Bishop dropped by to deliver some money to Justice. As he entered the loft, he heard Jamal shouting from his room, fighting hard in a game of NBA 2K.

Bishop's curiosity led him to ask if he could join. Jamal, excited to share the game, agreed. Since that day, they had spent more time together when the opportunity allowed. However, it was a secret kept from Justice. Neither Bishop nor

Jamal wanted her to know about their friendship, fearing her disapproval.

Bishop's influence was unmistakable, as Jamal talked differently and engaged in activities he wouldn't have considered before. He knew Justice wouldn't approve of their friendship, given Bishop's reputation as a quiet, grimy manipulator. If it were up to Justice, Jamal would be as far away from Bishop as possible, but the situation had taken a different turn.

The cold air nipped at Jamal's face as he hurried to the waiting Lamborghini truck. The luxurious, candy apple red vehicle stood out against the snowy backdrop, its tinted windows hinting at the hidden world inside.

Bishop was behind the wheel. He rolled down the window. "Hurry up, nigga!" His voice boomed.

Without hesitation, Jamal quickly darted to the back passenger side and climbed in. The plush interior was enveloped in a thick cloud of smoke as he entered.

"Here, hit this shit." Ox, seated in the front passenger seat, leaned back and passed Jamal the blunt. Jamal's disdain toward Ox, stemming from his inappropriate attention to Justice, had only grown. But he took the blunt anyway, determined not to appear weak or scared. He wanted to gain Bishop's acceptance, just as Ox had.

Jamal's attempt to take a hit from the blunt ended in a fit of coughs and watery eyes. Bishop and Ox filled the car with laughter as Jamal tried to regain his composure.

"What is this?" Jamal choked out, the potent high washing over him.

"That's that heme!" Ox laughed harder.

"What the fuck is that?" Jamal mumbled, his senses

becoming hazy as he reclined into the plush leather seat, struggling to maintain his calm.

"That's dust, nigga," Bishop clarified. "You got that wit' you?" he asked.

Lost in thought, Jamal stared into the distance momentarily. Then he snapped back to reality. "Oh, yeah," he said, reaching into his pants. He retrieved the unloaded gun he had taken from the closet, a secret he believed Justice was unaware of.

Bishop handed Jamal a plastic bag containing a box of bullets. With his hands trembling from the potent substance they had smoked and his nerves threatening to take over, Jamal loaded the bullets into the gun's magazine. His heart raced, but the act of assembling the weapon gave him a sense of invincibility, power, and he felt untouchable.

"You know what you doing wit' that lil' nigga?" Ox questioned. In Ox's eyes, Jamal was still green to the streets, lacking the experience that would grant him acceptance in their world. Justice, his only saving grace, largely influenced Ox's tolerance for Jamal. If not for her, he might have taken a more aggressive stance.

Jamal remained silent, sinking back into his seat, the pistol in his grasp, his eyes fixed on the passing scenery beyond the window. The weight of his choices lingering in the air as they continued down the highway.

The bass from Ox's favorite song boomed through the car's speakers, rattling the windows as they cruised down the highway. His excitement was clear as he cranked the volume up to ear-splitting levels.

With one hand on the wheel and a blunt in the other, Bishop glanced at the rearview mirror. His eyes locked with

Jamal's, and there was a silent understanding between them. Jamal, under the influence of PCP, realized it was time.

Using music as a cover, he cocked the gun slide, loading a bullet. The world seemed to blur as Jamal raised his arm, and with unsteady hands, placed the cold barrel of the gun on Ox's head.

Time seemed to stretch as a tense silence fell over the vehicle, and the car sped down the highway, a lethal secret hidden beneath the thumping beat of the music.

You could barely hear the shot, because the sound was so muffled that it blended into the beat, like a quiet snare drum that only Jamal and Bishop understood.

Ox, previously enjoying the music, now slumped in his seat. His head lolled against the window, life extinguished in an instant. The stain of his blood spread across the leather car seat.

Bishop, unfazed, remained focused on the road. The thick haze of smoke from the blunt enveloped the interior of the car, adding an almost dreamlike quality to the scene. With Ox's body beside them, they continued to cruise down the highway, the boundaries between reality and nightmare blurred by the magnitude of what they had just done.

The high of invincibility disappeared as soon as the gunshot echoed in the car. Fear and dread replaced the intoxication. Jamal's mind was a frantic whirlwind, each thought crashing into the next. He couldn't escape the memory of his father, the man who had been his anchor and mentor, now forever tied to this gruesome act. He thought about the mother he never had the chance to know and wondered if she would have been able to prevent this descent into hell. His sister, Justice, her face filled with disappointment and concern, haunted his thoughts.

Reflecting on the life he had once dreamed of, he couldn't help but feel how a single, irreversible action had obliterated that dream. All the moments and choices that had led him to this reality played on a loop in his mind, while the aftermath of his first murder clung to him like a shroud of guilt.

Night after night, as Jamal drifted to sleep, the gruesome vision of Ox's bloodied face continued to haunt his dreams. He would wake up in the dead of night, drenched in cold sweat, gasping for breath. The images were stuck in his mind and would not release their grip, replaying in horrifying detail. Each morning brought forth a hollowed version of himself, bearing the weight of a secret that grew heavier with each passing day. Jamal's waking hours became a war; the devil on his back whispering evil thoughts, while he fought to hide his inner turmoil from his sister, Justice. She had noticed the subtle changes in him, the distance, the restlessness, and her growing curiosity was yet another torment in Jamal's already tumultuous existence.

❦   7   ❦

Months drifted by like forgotten dreams, each day pushing Jamal further into the streets he'd never intended to explore. The vibrant aspirations of his father's encouragement were now clouded by the growing shadows of his involvement in criminal activities, all under the watchful eye of his new mentor, Bishop.

Jamal's evolution was obvious. The bright, innocent young man was fading away, replaced by a distant version of himself. The once sparkling light in his eyes was gone, lured away by the streets.

As the weeks passed, Jamal's name was ringing through the streets of Harlem. Robberies, shootings, and high-stakes heists became his currency. His reputation took shape, whispered in the hidden corners of the city's underbelly.

During Jamal's plunge into this deceitful world, Justice remained unaware of her brother's involvement. She was preoccupied with concealing her own criminal life from him. Her efforts to protect Jamal from the dangers of her secrets had made her blind to the reality of the dangers he was embracing.

FBI HEADQUARTERS: LAUREL, VIRGINIA

At the FBI headquarters, Agents Parker and Mills sat hunched over a cluttered desk, their faces tense with determination. The mystery surrounding the murder of DEA agent Eric Hayes was far from unraveling, but they had received a couple of faint rays of hope.

Agent Parker shuffled through a stack of papers and glanced at Agent Mills. "These prints, Samantha. It's a long shot, but we need to find the owner. They're pristine, no records in the database."

Agent Mills nodded. "The potential killer might have no fingerprints or any traceable identity."

The hum of the computers punctuated their exchange by analyzing data in the background. Facts, leads, and dead ends filled the room.

Parker reached for a file, pulling out a sheet of paper with the results of the ballistics test. "At least this might give us something to go on. The bullets were forty caliber rounds, fired from a Smith & Wesson forty caliber firearm."

Mills leaned back in her chair, letting out a weary sigh. "We need a lot more to make sense of all this, Rob. The shooter's identity, the motive... it's still a puzzle."

Silence filled the room as agents grasped the enormity of their task and the lurking dangers of their investigation.

RED BANK, NEW JERSEY

Ted Malinowski's cozy living room was filled with the aroma of his sandwich and the clinking of beer cans. A television broadcast broke the stillness, grasping Ted's attention. The news report was about the unsolved murder of a DEA agent in Virginia. A picture of a BMW flashed on the screen, and Ted's eyes narrowed as he studied it.

"That car," he mumbled to himself, struggling to place where he'd seen it before. The memory snapped into focus, and he jolted, spilling beer onto the already stained carpet.

"Shit!" Ted cursed, grabbing his smartphone. Scrolling through his contacts, he searched for Carl Richards' number. As the phone rang on the other end, he couldn't shake the anxiety gnawing at him.

"Hello?" the voice on the line answered.

"Hey, Carl..." Ted began, his voice tense with urgency.

"Hey, what's up, Ted?" Carl responded.

Ted didn't mince words. "I might have some information about that BMW. If you're not busy, I need you to come and check this out."

Carl didn't hesitate. "I'm on my way."

In recent days, a growing weariness had taken over Justice. She woke up each morning, heavy-lidded and drained. The throbbing of migraines was a constant companion throughout her days. Unbeknownst to her, the hustle and the life she led had exacted a toll on her body. Her diet had deteriorated, replaced by hurried, unhealthy meals, and the gym, once a refuge for her, had become a memory. Her finely tuned physique had suffered, eroding into a shadow of its former self.

Seated on the sofa, she had wrapped herself in a cozy throw blanket, her tired eyes fixed on the reality television shows playing on the screen. She struggled to keep herself awake, to escape the nagging weariness that tugged at her. The sound of the locks on the front door pulled her from the brink of sleep. She sat up, pretending she hadn't been dozing off.

As the door swung open, Justice's eyes met the sight of her brother Jamal entering, his footsteps heavy. Just a few paces behind him stood Bishop. A furrow formed on Justice's brow, a question hovering on the edge of her thoughts. *What was Bishop doing here with Jamal?* She wondered. Yet, she dismissed her curiosity, rationalizing their accidental meeting. Justice had been expecting Bishop's visit today; the only thing she didn't know was the time of his arrival.

With a push, she threw the cozy blanket aside, shaking off the drowsiness, and moved to greet her brother and Bishop, her face a mask of welcoming and curiosity, hiding the deeper layers of fatigue.

Justice greeted Jamal and Bishop with a forced smile. "Hey, you two," she said, attempting to appear lively. "What's going on?"

Jamal looked at his sister. He knew he couldn't tell her about the things he'd been doing with Bishop, so he kept it vague. "Not much, sis. Bishop and I just ran into each other outside."

Bishop nodded in agreement. "Yeah, just bumped in to him comin' up," he chimed in.

Justice gave a warm but somewhat skeptical nod. She still couldn't shake the uneasy feeling that something wasn't right.

"Well, it's good to see you both. You want something to eat or drink?"

Jamal and Bishop declined the offer, and Justice couldn't hide her relief. She led them to the living room, where they settled in for a casual conversation. Deep down, she wished she could tell Jamal the truth, warn him about the danger he was getting involved in, but the weight of her own secrets held her back.

As they talked, Justice continued to fight off the fatigue and headaches, trying to maintain the facade of normalcy. The strain of her double life was taking a toll on her well-being, but she knew she had to keep her true self hidden from her brother at all costs.

Back in Red Bank, New Jersey, Carl Richards, the Colonel of the New Jersey State Police, sat on a worn-out futon in Ted Malinowski's janky apartment. The room exuded the smell of stale cigarettes and was cluttered with takeout containers and beer cans. Ted, an aging cop with aspirations, sat across from Carl.

"You see that right there..." Ted pointed to his scribbled notes on his notepad. His finger traced the lines and circles he had drawn around crucial details. "Looks like a match to me. What you think?" he asked, proud of his findings.

Carl, his younger and more career-driven counterpart, leaned in to study the comparison between Ted's notes and the newly gained report about the BMW from the Virginia murder scene. He furrowed his brow, his fingers dancing over the documents as he weighed the evidence. "Humph," he mused, rubbing his chin, a sign that he was deep in thought. "I think we got something..." he declared.

Ted broke into a gratified grin. His dream may have been to reach the heights that Carl had, but he lacked the motivation. He had always respected Carl, even though his younger colleague had climbed the ladder faster. This moment felt like progress towards recognition. Carl snapped a photo of Ted's notes on his smartphone, a nod to modern policing methods, and rose from the couch.

"Aye," he said as he straightened his suit jacket before heading toward the door. "Clean this fuckin' place up. It's a goddamn pigsty in here... sheesh..." With those parting words, Carl exited the cluttered apartment, slamming the door behind him.

Justice parked her vehicle as close to the curb as she could, mindful of avoiding any damage to her precious rims. She shifted the car into park and waited for Bishop to exit the store. The crowded block felt deserted, and a weird sensation gnawed at Justice, though she couldn't quite pinpoint the cause. Her instincts were on high alert as she monitored her surroundings.

After what felt like forever, but was only 15 minutes, Justice spotted an unmarked car circling the block. Another suspicious presence revealed itself across the street, a vehicle with dark tinted windows stationed opposite the store where Bishop and his crew conducted their dealings. Justice made a mental note of the details, maintaining her heightened state of vigilance. Just as her impatience grew, Bishop emerged from the store.

Following Ox's murder, a dark cloud hovered over Bishop.

He had taken on an unsettling air, one that hinted at his involvement in the betrayal. Although he assured Ox's family and friends that he was out of town, doubt remained attached to him. Those on the streets who shared the block with Bishop couldn't shake the feeling that he was the ultimate double-crosser. They sensed the dark current in his demeanor, but they had nothing but their gut instincts and a growing conviction that Bishop had blood on his hands, as they were left without Ox's body.

He settled into the car and greeted Justice with a casual, "Whaddup, sis... Everything good?"

However, Justice's focus remained on the car across the street. "Whose car is that?"

Bishop scratched his head in confusion. "I don't know. It's been there for a few days," he confessed.

"A few days? And nobody bothered to check it out?" She pointed out the unmarked car as it circled the block once more.

Bishop, bemused, raised his shoulders. "I don't know, sis. We'll look into it. You good?" he asked, his voice carrying a hint of skepticism.

Justice looked into Bishop's eyes. "Did you take care of that?" she questioned.

His hesitation was clear as he turned away, looking out the window. He turned back to meet Justice's eyes. "Yeah. It's been handled."

"Why haven't I heard anything?"

"They haven't found the body. His people think he OT."

"Who you get to do it?" Justice asked, just as her phone rang. She asked Bishop to hold on, answering the call from Jamal. "What's up, little brother?" she greeted. After their brief conversation, she reassured Jamal, "I'll be home soon. Okay. See you in a few."

She turned back to Bishop and asked again, "So, who did it?"

The smirk that crept across Bishop's face set off alarm bells. "I had one of my young niggas handle it," he replied with a laugh.

As their conversation finished, Bishop exited the car, standing at the curb as Justice pulled away into the flowing traffic. The realization of how little she knew about these treacherous streets settled in his thoughts as he watched her disappear into the distance.

AN HOUR LATER

Justice sat in her loft, basking in the sheer emptiness of the room. Her phone pierced the silence, and she answered as Luck's number flashed on the screen. "Hello?"

"Feds just snatched Bishop," Luck's voice tensed on the other end.

Justice's eyes widened in disbelief. She struggled to find the right words but managed, "I just saw Bishop, Luck. I had a bad feeling on that block. I mentioned something was wrong, but he dismissed it. Shit!" Her anger boiled within, not so much about Bishop's arrest, but the reality that if they got him, they might be watching her too.

Luck's instructions cut through the chaos. "Meet me at the church in a hour," he said before ending the call.

Justice dropped the phone, and her mind was a tornado of worry and fear. The world she had built was crumbling around her, and a thousand thoughts raced through her head.

The front door creaked open, and Jamal stepped inside, oblivious to the turmoil that had consumed Justice. "Hey, sis," he greeted, his smile at odds with the tension in the room. Justice's pacing and visible distress caught his attention. "Justice, something's not right. You okay?" he asked, his voice reflecting his growing concern.

Justice turned to face her brother. "The feds just got Bishop..."

Darkness consumed the streets as Justice arrived at the cathedral. A chill ran down her spine as she stepped out of her car, the cold air nipping at her skin. She wrapped her fur coat tighter around herself and hurried towards the entrance.

As she pushed open the heavy cathedral doors, the silence inside was deafening. She couldn't help but feel a heavy weight in the air. Justice took a deep breath and ventured further in. All the people were seated at the back, their expressions tense, waiting. Luck's entire crew had gathered, their eyes fixed on her.

"I see you finally decided to show up," Luck's voice cut through the stillness as he addressed her.

"Caught a little traffic coming over the bridge. Did I miss anything?"

"Nah," Luck responded, his tone serious. "We were waiting for you."

Justice took a seat beside Keisha, a sense of foreboding hanging over the meeting.

Luck stood up, his presence commanding the room's attention. The dim cathedral seemed to fade away as he spoke.

"My people, you know these streets have eyes and ears. The feds, they're moving, and they're moving fast," Luck began.. "We're a family here, and I ain't about to let anything tear us apart. Our loyalty, our unity—it's what's kept us strong all this time."

He scanned the faces of his crew, their expressions focused, knowing that this was a pivotal moment.

"Now, as a family, we gotta look out for each other," he continued. "If you see something, if you hear something, you better share it. We can't afford secrets, not in this game."

As Luck spoke, his eyes fell on Keisha, and the room's atmosphere grew tense. He knew about the run-in at Walmart, and Keisha didn't know that her friend Kim had revealed it to him. He addressed her, his voice sharp and disapproving.

"Keisha, you think I don't know about that little incident at Walmart?" he said, his disappointment visible. "You kept it from me. You thought you could keep it a secret, but secrets don't last long on these streets."

Keisha's face blanched as the room's attention focused on her. Luck's rebuke stung, and she felt exposed.

"You and I share blood," Luck continued. "You should've told me. We in this shit together, for better or worse. You keeping secrets, that's a stab in the back to us all. I'm disappointed in you, sis."

He paused, his eyes moving to each member of his crew. "With Bishop in the feds' hands, we can't afford to trust anything. We need to be suspicious of everything—watch your backs and each other's. We can't let his arrest unravel us, especially if he's talking. That's a line we can't cross."

The silence in the cathedral was suffocating as Keisha tried to collect herself, realizing the gravity of her mistake and the consequences it could bring to their tight-knit family. And as Luck's speech resonated with everyone present, they understood that their world had become even more dangerous. The stakes had never been higher.

After giving his sermon, Luck waited for the others to clear out, leaving him alone with Justice. As they settled into two empty pews, he took a deep breath, his eyes filled with memories of a past he shared.

"Justice, you ever wonder how I got into all this?" he began. "You see, I didn't have a family to call my own. My mom, she was addicted to that poison, and she couldn't take care of me."

Justice stared at him, absorbing every word. She knew he was about to reveal something personal.

"State took me away, put me in a bunch of group homes, institutions," Luck continued, his eyes fixed on an invisible horizon. "They were supposed to be my 'family.' But all they did was teach me how to survive, the only way I knew how."

He leaned in closer to her, his voice filled with emotion. "The first time I killed someone... it wasn't planned. It was him or me, Justice. Life was like that in those places. I took that step, and it changed me forever."

Justice felt the pain of his confession, understanding the darkness that had shaped him.

Luck's eyes locked onto hers. "Justice, we've been building something here. You and me. I see you as a leader. The backbone. But Keisha, my flesh and blood, she betrayed us. She kept secrets and lied to me. Secrets that could unravel everything we've worked so hard for."

His words hung in the air, heavy with the weight of the ultimatum he was about to deliver. "Justice, I need you to do something you won't like, something I won't like. But it's a choice we make to protect this family."

Justice's heart sank, knowing the burden of what he was asking. She nodded, her voice above a whisper. "What do you need me to do, Luck?"

As the cathedral's shadows deepened around them, the weight of their world was crushing, pushing them further into a darkness they had embraced.

Luck looked into Justice's eyes. "I need you to kill Keisha." he said.

Justice didn't know what to do. *Kill Keisha?* She thought to herself. *Nah.* "That's your sister..." she replied, but the look in Luck's eyes told her a different story. She knew he was dead ass serious. "Why me?" she asked.

"It has to be you because you're the one I trust most. You've got the heart and the nerve to do what needs to be done for this family."

Justice felt a sinking feeling in the pit of her stomach. She was always loyal to Luck and the crew, but this request exceeded her wildest expectations. "But it's your sister, Luck. Blood."

"Sometimes, family ain't just about blood. It's about loyalty, about trust. You and I, we've been through similar situations. We've got our own kind of family here, one that we built from the ground up."

Torn between her loyalty to Luck and the love for her friend, Justice's voice wavered as she spoke. "I need time. This... it ain't something I can rush into."

Luck nodded, understanding the gravity of what he had asked. "Take the time you need, but don't forget what's at stake here. I'll give you the space to think about it."

As they left the cathedral, the chill in the night air mirrored the cold decision that lingered between them. Justice's heart ached, knowing that in the coming days, she'd face a choice that could tear her apart.

Deep within the heart of the federal investigation, Agent Samantha Wells and Agent Robert Parker worked overtime, their every move methodical and strategic. They sat in a cramped office, surrounded by an array of photographs, charts, and surveillance tapes.

"We've got to crack this, Samantha," Agent Parker mumbled as he scribbled notes on a legal pad. "Luck's operation is huge, and it's more complex than we thought."

Samantha agreed, her fingers dancing across a keyboard, searching for any digital breadcrumbs that might lead them closer to their target. "We're dealing with a formidable adversary, and he's surrounded by loyal associates."

Their investigation had already yielded valuable clues and leads: intercepted phone conversations, bank transactions, and witness testimonies. They knew that Luck was at the center of a criminal empire that spanned drugs, extortion, and financial fraud, among other activities.

Looking at the evidence board, Samantha realized a crucial puzzle piece was absent. "We need to turn someone close to Luck, someone who'll give us the inside scoop."

Agent Parker leaned back in his chair, staring at a map of key locations related to the operation. "We need a chink in the armor, Sam. We're close. We just need that one break."

While piecing together the puzzle, the agents were aware of

the ruthless challenge and high stakes. They couldn't afford to make any mistakes. They had not yet finished the fight to dismantle Luck's criminal empire, but they remained strong in their resolve to see it through.

Keisha sat in a corner of the small Westchester County restaurant, her tea cooling as her mind raced. Her hands caressed her swollen belly as she thought about the life growing inside of her. She was on a mission, but it wasn't one that her brother, Luck, had approved of.

When Keisha first discovered her pregnancy, Luck had insisted that she lie low, tend to her maternal duties, and allow him to handle the street business. But Keisha had always been independent and determined to create her own path. She had continued to accumulate wealth from her successful exploits with fraudulent checks and online banking scams, operating in her own world, where she answered to no one.

Keisha Beckford had built an empire based on fraudulent schemes that spanned the digital realm. She was a master of check fraud, online banking scams, cryptocurrency cons, and an array of digital deceptions. With these endeavors, she raked in hundreds of thousands of dollars each week, all of which contributed to Luck's operation.

While her brother was incarcerated, she had chosen to go down this path, and when he returned, Luck sought a piece of the action. He used his connections and resources to help her expand her criminal enterprise. This lifestyle brought Keisha luxury beyond imagination, from high-end vehicles to designer clothing, bags, and shoes. Her existence seemed to be a dream, but the encounter with federal agents and her friend Kim at Walmart had thrust her once-perfect world into disarray. The walls were closing in, and Keisha could feel the ground beneath her shifting.

As she sat there, calculating the profits that would soon swell her accounts, a calm, authoritative voice shattered her thoughts.

"It's unfortunate that we must meet on these terms, Miss Beckford..." Agent Samantha Wells declared, her presence filling the space across from Keisha.

Agent Parker stood at Agent Wells' side, their presence spelling trouble. The prospect of her contact never arriving replaced Keisha's initial relief with a desire to disappear. Her heart pounded as Agent Parker placed five fraudulent checks on the table, a reminder that her illegal actions had not gone unnoticed.

"Expecting these?" he inquired. "Your friend won't be making it today. Instead, you've got us. Are you ready to talk?" The room seemed to close in on Keisha as she dealt with the enormity of the choice before her.

"What do you want?" Keisha said, her voice trembling as she realized the dire straits she was in.

Agent Wells, with a calm and measured demeanor, reached for Keisha's cup of tea, took a sip, and placed it back on the table. "We want to know the details about your brother's operation and his connections," she stated.

"I'm not at liberty to speak about something I know nothing about," Keisha lied, her anxiety growing by the second.

Agent Parker, sporting a sly smile, played the game Keisha was attempting. "Each one of those checks carries a minimum seven-year federal sentence in a federal institution. I've only shown you the five I have here. That's thirty-five years. But there's more where those came from, Miss Beckford. How would you like your child to be born in a federal prison?" His words hovered in the air like a dark cloud, adding to Keisha's growing distress.

Keisha contemplated the consequences of what Agent Parker had just told her. The thought of prison was unimaginable for her, and giving birth behind bars was one of her scariest situations. But Keisha was also aware of the repercussions she'd face if she said anything about her brother's operations.

"I can't talk about anything," she stated. "Luck would have me killed."

"We'll protect you, Keisha," Agent Wells promised.

Agent Parker chimed in. "You can trust us. Just tell us everything you know. We'll ensure your safety."

Keisha dropped her head, her emotions in turmoil. She had to walk a tightrope, undecided on which side to fall.

$$\approx \quad 8 \quad \approx$$

Keisha sat in the makeshift interrogation room of the restaurant. A tornado of emotions raged inside of her. Fear and loyalty went to war in her mind, each vying for dominance. Her unborn child symbolized an innocent future, yet complicated her decision. She contemplated exposing her brother's operation for the sake of her unborn child's future. However, the loyalty she had for Luck, her older brother and the only family she had left, countered that desire. Crossing him was something she feared, knowing the brutal reaction it might bring. Stakes were high, each choice a step into an unknown land with no clear exit. She looked between the agents, her lips sealed tight with the unsaid words that played back in her mind.

Agent Wells looked at Keisha. "We understand your predicament. Your loyalty to your brother is commendable, but your child's future shouldn't be marred by the choices of the past. We can provide protection, ensure your safety."

Agent Parker chimed in, "Let's be clear. We're not here to destroy families, but we must put a stop to this operation. Help us do that, and we'll make sure you get a chance at a normal life, away from the nonsense."

Keisha squirmed in her chair. "I wanna believe you, but it's... Luck, he... he's got his ways of finding out things. He'll know it was me."

Agent Wells responded, "We've dealt with sensitive cases before. We'll make sure you're safe, Keisha. Witness protection, new identity, everything. But you have to help us. This operation is causing harm to too many people."

Agent Parker's tone turned more earnest. "We're not looking to take you down. We want to dismantle this organization and stop more harm from spreading. With or without you, we will bring them to justice."

Keisha felt the promise of a safer life, but guilt lingered. She hesitated, unable to decide the course of her and her unborn child's future.

As she sat at the table, struggling with the agents' appeals, her mind drifted back to a memory. She recalled the day Luck was arrested and the burden of responsibility that fell on her shoulders. Keisha was out of her teens, entrusted with sustaining their family's finances. She remembered the panic and helplessness, the fear of their mother's disappointment, and the desperation to make ends meet. It was during those days she discovered her knack for manipulation, her sharp wit aiding her in many fraudulent activities.

In a dark room, enveloped in the glow of a computer screen, she remembered the rush that surged through her veins as she cracked a complex security system. That night, as she drained a significant sum of money from a corrupt corporation's bank accounts, she felt invincible. She recalled the sense of power, the freedom it offered, the ability to control her destiny. It was the first time she tasted success on her own terms.

Keisha's involvement in various schemes was set in motion at that moment. She thought about how far she had come since that night. The flashback brought back the fear of those times, the uncertainties that haunted her every waking moment. A single mother to-be, she felt like history was repeating itself. *Would her child face the same fate?*

Agent Parker's frustration was building. He'd had enough. "Okay, let's try this," he said, and slammed a photograph onto the table. "Do you know who this is?"

Keisha's heart raced as she stared at the picture of Bishop. She didn't believe the possibility of him betraying Luck, but the agents' words played back in her head with a disconcerting certainty. It was a nerve-wracking revelation that threatened to shatter her trust in the people she thought she knew.

"Are you saying he's cooperating?" Keisha whispered.

Agent Wells' eyes locked with Keisha. "If you've got information, now is the time to share it. Don't let someone else control your destiny, Keisha."

"We won't let you rot in prison if you help us." Agent Parker assured.

Keisha's mind was in shambles. Bishop's involvement had opened a new chapter of uncertainty in her life. Betraying her brother meant betraying the one person who had protected her for years, but what the agents were telling her presented an even more terrifying prospect — the idea that Bishop might have already unraveled the secrets of their world.

As she stared at Bishop's photograph, the weight of her decision felt like a thousand pounds. It wasn't just about her loyalty to her brother, Luck, or the consequences she might face. The stakes were far higher—her unborn child's future hung in the balance, along with the fate of her family.

Keisha's fearful eyes didn't escape Agent Wells, who emphasized the gravity of the situation. "Keisha, we understand this is difficult, but you're not just making this choice for yourself. You're making it for your child, too. Can you imagine your baby growing up behind bars or constantly fearing for their safety?"

"The longer you stay silent, the more dangerous this situation becomes." Agent Parker added. "Your cooperation can ensure a safer future for you and your family."

With trembling hands, Keisha felt the room closing in. She knew that her decision would affect the lives of everyone she loved. Despite her heavy heart, she had to choose between her loyalty and her family's future.

"What do you wanna know?" She said.

As the words left her lips, a slow, knowing smile spread across Agents Parker and Wells' faces. They had broken through her resistance, and the secrets she held were about to unfold.

Keisha had made her choice, and now she would disclose the intricate web of criminal activities, connections, and secrets she had kept hidden for so long. The road ahead was uncertain, but one thing was clear: her cooperation would have far-reaching consequences for the world she had known and the lives entangled in its complex web.

Darren Lindsey didn't budge in the face of the federal charges. He leaned back in his chair as the interrogation room filled up with cigarette smoke. The federal agent across the table persisted, but Darren wasn't having any of it. He took a long drag from his cigarette, exhaling.

"Listen, motherfucka," Darren growled, blowing out smoke through his nostrils. "I ain't got shit to say, so y'all can send me wherever the fuck you gon' send me. I got lawyer money."

The agent's frustration was clear, but he realized Darren was unbreakable. He lived by the streets' code and never crossed the line of snitching. Despite the dire circumstances, he clung to his dignity and loyalty, prepared to face whatever consequences lay ahead.

Darren Lindsey, known on the streets as Bishop, was born and raised in the gritty neighborhoods of the Bronx, New York. From a young age, he held a unique charisma that drew people to him, often masking the crazy lifestyle he was born into. Adversity and hardship characterized Bishop's early life, and as he grew older, he walked a path alongside his partner in crime, Ox.

Bishop and Ox were a duo, infamous for terrorizing the streets of New York City. They robbed anything and anyone that crossed their path. Bishop's charm and wit complemented Ox's brute force, a dynamic that earned them notoriety and respect in the criminal underworld. Bishop may have had charisma, but it was Ox who instilled fear in everyone.

Their crime-wave spanned years, and the duo left a trail of anguish, destruction, and blood in their wake. They flourished in a world of violence and deception, and Bishop learned to survive by any means necessary. For a time, it seemed like they were unstoppable, taking what they wanted and leaving behind a wake of devastation.

However, as Bishop's journey unfolds, their reign couldn't

last forever. A chess move was made, and Bishop faced a decision. He had to kill Ox, the man he'd stood side by side with for so long. This left a hole in Bishop's soul, a wound that he could never heal.

The traumatic event forever altered Bishop's life, and the weight of his past decisions continued to haunt him. Now, facing the prospect of cooperating with the law to avoid a lengthy prison sentence, Bishop struggled with his sense of loyalty and the knowledge that there could be no redemption for his past sins. His journey was one of tragedy, conflict, and self-discovery, and it would determine his fate.

The aroma of fresh coffee hung in the air as Ted and Carl sat in their usual corner booth, the morning sunlight streaming through the cafe windows. Carl took a thoughtful sip of his coffee, his eyes locked on Ted's. "You wouldn't believe what I found, Ted. That BMW you pulled over? It's a match for the murder of DEA agent Eric Hayes."

Ted's eyes widened. "You serious? That's the same car?"

Carl nodded. "I did some digging, and the registered owner is a woman named Keisha Beckford. Now, that name ring any bells?"

Ted scratched his head, deep in thought. "Keisha... Beckford? Sounds familiar, but I can't put a face to it."

Carl leaned in, his voice lowered. "This is where it gets interesting. I cross-referenced the details, and she's tied to some guy named Lucian, the head of a major criminal operation. We stumbled onto something big here."

"So, what happens now?" Ted asked.

"I made a few calls. I'm waiting on this guy, Agent Robert Parker, to call me back," Carl replied, his eyes scanning the cafe as if expecting someone to emerge at any moment.

Ted leaned back, running his fingers through his hair. "Parker? That's federal territory, Carl. This is bigger than what we usually handle."

Carl nodded. "I know, Ted. But if this Keisha is connected to Lucian and they're involved in something as serious as a DEA agent's murder, we might be in over our heads. We need federal help on this one."

The tension in the booth thickened as Ted absorbed the gravity of the situation. The clinking of cutlery and the low chatter of conversations around them blurred into the background as they faced the implications of their unexpected discovery.

On a cold winter evening, Justice cruised through the blocks of her old neighborhood. The sight of the house where she, her brother and her father had once lived triggered a flood of memories. Despite a new family occupying it, vivid recollections lingered like past ghosts.

With no destination in mind, Justice contemplated the task at hand. It wasn't the act of taking someone's life that unsettled her; it was the identity of the person Luck had asked her to kill. Keisha was a longtime friend who had supported Justice, especially during challenging times. Keisha's generosity had played a pivotal role in Justice's current lifestyle.

Contemplating the severity of the situation, Justice fought conflicting emotions. Keisha wasn't just an acquaintance; she was a friend who had come through for her in times of need. Now, faced with an order that contradicted their history, Justice struggled to compartmentalize their friendship and view the task as just a business obligation. It proved to be a daunting feat, testing her ability to prioritize self-preservation over a deep, personal connection.

Amid her internal conflict, Justice understood the consequences of defying Luck's orders. Her own fate was in question, causing her to suppress her emotions and focus on the choices before her.

Lost in her thoughts and unaware of her destination, Justice finds herself on the same street where her late father's barbershop stands. An unexpected impulse takes over her, prompting her to pull up in front of the establishment. It had been years since she set foot inside, having entrusted the business to her father's partner, Derrick, after his passing. Circumstances forced her hand, leaving her with no choice but to relinquish control.

As she parked in front of the shop, Justice noticed the lights were still on, a surprising sight. She peeked through the window. Inside, only two people occupied the space—the dubious business partner and a man engaged in conversation while seated in the barber chair. Without hesitation, Justice entered.

The once-thriving business, a source of pride for her father, now carried signs of neglect. She glanced around, realizing the missing vibrant ambiance. It was a reminder of the changes life had undergone since her father's passing.

"I see you managed to turn this into a shit hole," Justice remarked, her words cutting through the air and catching Derrick off guard.

He turned, his initial surprise melting into a hesitant recognition. "Justice?"

"Yea, it's me," she confirmed, her presence sending a ripple of discomfort through the neglected barbershop. "What happened to this place?"

Derrick, feeling defensive, retorted, "Humph, you got some fuckin' nerve coming into my establishment and disrespecting me in front of my face. I know your father taught you better than that."

The mention of her father struck a nerve, and Justice's anger bubbled to the surface. "Leave my father out of this. Because you and I know if he were here, none of this," she gestured around, "would be happening." The exchange was the result of years of neglect and unfulfilled expectations.

"Yeah, well... he ain't here. And what do you want, anyway?" Derrick asked, his patience wearing thin from Justice's direct approach.

"I'm here to make you a business proposal."

"Business?" Derrick laughed, shaking his head. "Me and you, we ain't got no business."

"I want to buy you out, Derrick," Justice declared. "You're running this shop into the ground, and I'm giving you the opportunity to at least make a few dollars from all of this."

Derrick laughed again. "You hear this shit, Lee?" he said to the man sitting in the barber chair next to him. "This little bitch said she gon' give me an opportunity... ain't that some shit?"

"Ignorance is a costly luxury. Letting a chance like this slip through your fingers is like watching your dreams evaporate in the smoke of your own ignorance," Justice replied. Spending time around Luck was rubbing off on her.

Derrick exchanged a glance with Lee. Uncertainty covered both of their faces. "You can take your opportunity and stick it up your ass for all I care. Now get the fuck outta here."

A torrent of anger accompanied Derrick's outright rejection of Justice's proposal. The hostility was thick, and for Justice, it felt like the ghosts of the past were closing in.

Her demeanor shifted from composed to commanding as she backed out a shiny nine-millimeter handgun from her fur coat. A wicked smile played on her lips as she leveled the gun at Derrick, who, in an instant, went from defiance to sheer panic. "Whoa! Whoa! Hold up! Hold up... I didn't mean it like that," he pleaded. "Let's talk about this," he stammered.

But Justice maintained a steady aim, her eyes focused like a seasoned marksman. "I tried talking; that didn't seem to work."

Derrick's cries echoed in the barbershop as he pleaded for mercy, hands raised in surrender. Meanwhile, Lee, sitting in the barber chair, remained unreadable, unfazed by the escalating tension. Beneath his composed exterior, Lee harbored a readiness to kill, a relic of his old-school gangster days in the '70s. His presence in the barbershop wasn't just coincidental; he had a score to settle. Derrick owed him money. Lee's calm demeanor masked the anticipation of a predator, poised to strike at the slightest hint of vulnerability from Justice.

General Lee Dunbar, a seasoned veteran of the Vietnam War, emerged from the battlefield only to find himself entangled in the gritty streets of New York. Haunted by the traumas of war, he sought pleasure in the numbing embrace of the wonder drug, opium, a habit that held him tight on his return home. Faced with the truth that the government offered no respite, General Lee, like many others, navigated the post-war streets, battling addiction and survival. In a moment of self-discovery, he made a choice to break free from the chains of substance abuse, transitioning from user to purveyor.

Embracing the streets with a new purpose, General Lee capitalized on his international connections, transforming himself into a force in the drug trade. The birth of the General's Crew marked a notorious era spanning from the early eighties to the mid-nineties. They were infamous for murder and extortion, and General Lee had earned a reputation as a black millionaire in Harlem, leaving his mark on the landscape of the city.

The gunshot was loud as Derrick collapsed to the floor. Without a moment's pause, Justice redirected the barrel toward Lee, perched in the barber chair, undisturbed by the violence. "Who are you?" She demanded.

Lee's smile persisted. He looked down at Derrick's body before returning to meet Justice's eyes. "Back in the days when the corners spoke louder than words, I earned mine with lead and loyalty. They labeled me a villain, but in these streets, I'm the reaper collecting dues, and you just took on his debt..." he told her. Lee's calm voice carried an ominous weight as he rose from the barber chair. Passing by Justice, he headed toward the exit without a glance back, leaving behind the aftermath of a deadly transaction.

The Porsche tore down the highway like a bullet, the wind howling in Jamal's ears as they left a trail of blood in their wake. Unbeknownst to them, the eyes of an NYPD officer in his patrol car observed their daredevil escapade. The patrol car's lights ignited, painting the night in a kaleidoscope of red and blue.

Seeing the threat in his rearview mirror, Jamal responded with an extra dose of horsepower, pushing the speedometer past the century mark. The pursuit transformed the highway into a racing speedway, the patrol car chasing like a shadow while the helicopters hovered above.

After 17 adrenaline-fueled minutes, Jamal attempted to exit the highway, only to collide with the median. The impact ejected the front seat passenger through the windshield, a tragic casualty of their reckless flight. In the aftermath, Jamal and the surviving passenger found themselves in cuffs, the spoils of their venture—50 pounds of marijuana and a pair of handguns—confiscated by the police.

Shackled to a hospital bed, Jamal's mind raced faster than the highway they had just left. Thoughts of his late father, a distant but haunting presence, flashed in his mind. *How would his old man react to the wreckage of his son's life?* Jamal, struggling with the oncoming storm of Justice's wrath, pushed the thought from his head.

His body ached from the impact of the crash, but the pain was nothing compared to what he had to face from Justice.

Silence filled the hospital room until the door creaked open, and Justice entered, her expression a mix of anger and concern. Her eyes locked onto Jamal, who tried to muster a smile that fell flat.

"Jamal, what the fuck happened?"

Jamal hesitated, searching for the right words. "It's a long story, Sis. But we got caught up in a chase with the NYPD. Things went left."

Justice's eyes narrowed. "Chase? NYPD? Are you out of your mind, Jamal?" She paced the room, her frustration escalating. "You gotta be kidding me. Dad would go crazy if he saw you like this."

Jamal winced at the mention of their father. "I know. I fucked up. But we had the product, and I thought I could…"

"Thought you could, what, impress your friends? You know who you stole from, right? Pedro Remirez, Jamal. The fuckin' Mexican cartel! They don't play games. They'll come after you, after us."

Jamal's eyes got wide, and a cold sweat broke out on his forehead. "The Mexican cartel? Shit, I didn't know. We just thought it was a easy vic."

Justice shook her head. "Easy vic? Nothing's easy when you're dealing with cartels. Do you even understand the shit you've dragged us into?"

The hospital room door creaked open again. Luck stood there, his expression cold and calculating. His eyes locked onto Jamal. The room felt smaller.

"Who the fuck is he?" Jamal asked, his confusion clear.

Justice shot Jamal a warning look. "Jamal, this is Luck."

Jamal's eyes widened in realization, and then a smirk played on his lips. "Luck? So, you're the big shot. The one the streets can't stop talkin' about."

"And you must be Jamal. The one who thinks playin' with the cartel is a smart move."

"I don't need a lecture from some nigga I don't know. I run my own shit."

Luck stepped closer. "You're running your shit into a grave, kid. Stealing from Pedro Ramirez? You got no idea who you fuckin' with."

Jamal shot back, "Fuck em..."

"Guys, we have bigger problems." Justice cut in. "The Ramirez cartel is after Jamal, and we need a plan to deal with it."

Luck's eyes never left Jamal. "You got yourself in some deep shit, and now it's my problem, too. You owe me an explanation for this."

"I don't owe you shit..." Jamal replied.

"Jamal, you need to understand. Since Dad died, I've been working with Luck. He's been looking out for us. The apartment, the car..."

Jamal's eyes moved between Justice and Luck, the realization sinking in. "What? You been workin' with this nigga all this time, and you never told me?"

"Seems like there's a lot you don't know, kid," Luck said. "And a lot you're about to find out."

❦ 9 ❦

In the Metropolitan Correctional Center (MCC) in Manhattan, Bishop remained in federal custody. His predicament unfolded through repeated courtroom rituals. Twice denied bail, the reasons remained elusive. Frustration was at its peak, accentuated by the bewilderment mirrored in his lawyer's eyes. He was unable to offer any clarity.

Back in the interrogation room, the images of Ox's bloody body poked Bishop's senses. The federal agent held the photograph before him, his eyes fixed on the brutal aftermath of violence. "You know who that is?"

Bishop's jaw clenched. The image was a betrayal of the street code, a breach of the unspoken rules that governed their world. His eyes were now clouded with a storm of conflicting emotions. Ox, his partner in crime, the one he'd ran the streets with, lay there in a pool of his own blood. The reality hit Bishop like a tidal wave, drowning him in a sea of remorse and anger.

The agent pressed on. "We found him, and we can add a murder charge to your growing list of offenses. Your loyalty to the streets just cost you even more, Darren."

The weight of a potential life sentence for murder pressed on Bishop's shoulders. "That's not my work," he responded. The air in the room was heavy with uncertainty as he struggled with the idea of cooperation, a notion that seemed foreign and repugnant.

The federal agent was unmoved. "Well, whose work is it?" The question hung in the air. It wasn't just about his actions; it was about the allegiance he would choose in a world where loyalties were fickle and alliances were often a shifting landscape. The room held its breath, awaiting Bishop's decision—a decision that could alter his life.

Bishop, caught in the crossroads of his own fate, dared to broach the pivotal question. "What's in it for me?"

"Nothing's promised. But I can almost guarantee you won't do life for this murder."

As Bishop weighed his options, the room retained its sterile facade, masking the high-stakes negotiations that played out in the shadows.

The highway stretched ahead, a ribbon of asphalt cutting through the night. In the confines of Carl's Ford pickup truck, the sound of the engine provided a steady rhythm to the conversation between NJ State troopers, Carl Richards, and Ted Malinowski. The road signs flashed by, indicating the miles ticking away as they neared the rendezvous point in Virginia.

"I can't believe we're making this drive," Ted remarked, glancing at the navigation screen spread across the dashboard.

Carl laughed, his eyes focused on the road. "Sometimes, you've got to go where the leads take you. And right now, they're pointing south."

As they crossed into Virginia, the city lights on the horizon signaled their approach. The pickup pulled into a designated meeting spot, and there, under the pale streetlights, agents Robert Parker and Samantha Mills awaited them. They stepped forward as they parked, handshakes and nods of recognition exchanged in the cool night air.

"Carl, Ted," Parker greeted, his tone serious but determined. "This is my partner, agent Mills. Let's cut to it. What have you got for us?"

The four of them huddled, exchanging details and insights. The night held the weight of anticipation, and as they delved into the heart of their findings, the investigation spread, reaching deeper into the unknown.

Agent Parker scrutinized the notes Ted handed him, the details scattered out before him like pieces of a puzzle snapping into place. He nodded thoughtfully. "Looks like a match to me," he affirmed, passing the notes over to Agent Mills.

Agent Mills reviewed the information with a discerning eye. "This is significant. It's something we've been searching for," she acknowledged.

Ted, eager to contribute, interjected, "And that's not all. We traced the registration back to a... What's the name, Carl?" Ted turned to his partner, momentarily blanking on the crucial detail.

Carl looked at his notepad. "A Miss Keisha Beckford. The

registration is linked to a female by that name. You familiar with her?"

The federal agents exchanged a look, their eyes widening in sync. In unison, they exclaimed, "Keisha Beckford!"

Ted, oblivious to the depth of his revelation, pressed for more. "You guys know her?"

The agents struggled to contain their astonishment. "Yes, we do know of a Keisha Beckford," Agent Parker finally responded.

As the two agents and the troopers discussed the evidence, agent Mills's phone interrupts the discussion. "Excuse me, guys, I need to take this," she said, stepping aside. "Agent Mills speaking. Uh-huh. You've got to be kidding me. Are you sure? Okay. We'll be there within the next twenty-four hours. Thank you," she said, ending the call. She turned back to the group. "You won't believe the call I just got."

Agent Parker inquired, "Who was it?"

"That was the NYC district attorney's office. Apparently, they've got a gun that matches the ballistics of the weapon used in the murder of DEA agent Eric Hayes."

Their eyes widened, and their mouths hung open in aston-ishment.

NYC CRIMINAL COURT: 100 CENTER STREET

The courtroom was filled with whispers as Jamal stood there, waiting, his eyes moving between his lawyer, Miss Crystal Haden, and the stern-faced judge presiding over the case. Miss Haden, a reputable figure in the legal world, exuded an air of confidence, but even she couldn't conceal her concern at the unexpected turn of events.

As the judge began to recite Jamal's charges, anticipation swept through the room. However, the proceeding was disrupted when the district attorney requested a private conversation at the bench, prompting Miss Haden to join them.

"Your honor, with all due respect, this case has just gone federal," the district attorney announced.

"Federal?" Miss Haden questioned.

The DA proceeded to unveil the shocking revelation—the discovery of a firearm in Jamal's possession that matched the murder weapon used in the killing of a DEA agent in Virginia.

"Virginia?" The simultaneous gasps from both Miss Haden and the judge underscored the gravity of the situation. The DA substantiated his claim with a stack of evidence, and as Miss Haden reviewed the documents, a shadow of realization crossed her face.

"I'll need a few moments to talk this over with my client, your honor," Miss Haden requested, her legal acumen already calculating the intricate dance she would need to perform in this sudden, high-stakes federal arena.

"Take as much time as you need. I'll call a recess until two PM," the judge declared, his gavel punctuating the gravity of the situation.

In the confined space of the consultation room, Miss Haden pressed Jamal for answers. "What is this about the murder of a DEA agent in Virginia?" she probed.

Jamal, however, seemed genuinely baffled. "Virginia? Murder? DEA? I don't know anything about none of that," he insisted, the weight of the accusation alien to him.

Just as Miss Haden prepared to delve deeper into Jamal's predicament, the door swung open, revealing the unexpected entrance of Justice and Luck. The atmosphere changed, and tension grew in the room.

"What's going on with this case?" Justice's eyes scanned Miss Haden for answers.

The lawyer shook her head. "The DA says one of the guns found in Jamal's possession was used in the murder of a DEA agent in Virginia."

Justice exchanged a glance with Luck.

"I don't know what the hell they're talking about, Justice..." Jamal protested, his voice laced with desperation as he caught the subtle exchange between the two of them. "What the fuck y'all got me into?"

"Miss Haden, can you give us a minute, please?" Luck asked.

"Sure. I'll leave you guys to talk this over." Miss Haden gracefully exited, leaving Justice, Luck, and Jamal to confront the mystery that had woven itself around them.

Jamal, still in the dark, sought answers. "What's going on here? Somebody gon' tell me somethin'?"

Justice, taking charge, pulled out a chair and settled in front of him. "Where'd you get that gun, Jamal?"

"What gun?"

"The gun you got caught with."

Trapped in the web of his own actions, Jamal hesitated, but eventually spilled the truth. "I took it out of the closet," he admitted.

Justice mulled over his words. Then, suddenly, the pieces clicked into place, and her expression shifted. "The closet?" She mumbled to herself, connecting the dots. It hit her—the gun had been stashed away when they first moved into the loft. Despite her initial intention to dispose of it, the passage of time and life's chaos caused it to fade into the recesses of her memory. "Oh shit..." she uttered, realizing with the weight of her oversight.

"You kept that shit?" Luck's question sliced through the room.

"I meant to get rid of it, but I forgot..."

Jamal, still facing with the weight of his actions, questioned the conversation unfolding before him. "What are y'all talkin' about?"

"You weren't supposed to touch that, Jamal," she said. "What did you need a gun for?"

Jamal, sensing that the truth was his only ally, decided to lay it all bare. "I had to do somethin' for Bishop," he confessed.

The mention of Bishop sent a shiver down Justice's spine. She feared Jamal was referring to a dark chapter she desperately wished to keep closed. "Bishop?" she probed, her mind racing. "What did you do for Bishop, Jamal?"

Unable to look at his sister, Jamal dropped his head. It became evident that the truth he was about to reveal had the power to unravel the threads holding their world together.

"Bishop told me Ox was no good... so..."

Justice stood up, her movements agitated as she paced the floor. "No... tell me you didn't do that, Jamal. Please... no..." she pleaded, the desperation evident in her voice.

Jamal locked eyes with his sister, tears streaming down his cheeks. "I did it for you, sis..." His voice cracked with emotion. "Bishop said Ox was gonna bring everybody down and that he was a thief. He said he had to go."

"Bishop had to go?" Luck questioned, his disbelief evident. As far as he knew, Bishop was out of town with some of his family.

Justice turned to Luck for answers. "You told Keisha Bishop had to go. Didn't you?"

"You killed Bishop?" In a surge of anger, Luck lunged towards Jamal, grabbing him by the shirt collar.

"Luck, stop!" Justice cried out, tears streaming down her face. "Keisha came to me and said you gave the green light on Bishop. Said he was disloyal."

Luck released his grip on Jamal's collar. "I never told Keisha no shit like that..." he said.

In silence, they stood frozen, eyes locked in a web of emotions. No words were spoken, only thoughts drifting in the air. The bonds that once held them together now strained under the pressure of secrets and betrayals, leaving a mark on the fabric of their relationship.

Jamal's desperation filled the room. "Listen, I don't know what's going on, but I need to get outta here, Justice. Please... get me outta here." It was evident that Rikers Island wasn't a place Jamal was prepared for; the strain of the environment showed on him.

After glancing at Luck, Justice redirected her attention to her brother. "Jamal, we're in deep. Real deep. But I'll see what I can do. You need to stay calm, alright?" Her attempt at reassurance couldn't fully conceal the uncertainty that lingered beneath the surface. Rikers Island was a dangerous maze, and navigating its complexities demanded a delicate balance of alliances and street smarts that Jamal lacked.

"Stay calm? Justice, these dudes are animals in here. Please... you gotta get me outta here..." he begged.

Luck, assessing the situation, stepped forward to offer some assurance. "I'll see what I can do. Where you housed?"

"ESH."

"I'ma have somebody come see you. Just be cool. Everything gon' be alright." Luck's words carried a sort of comfort, and Jamal, though still tense, felt a bit of hope. In the gritty environment of Rikers Island, Luck's reputation and influence could make a significant difference.

The city lights flickered in the distance as Justice and Luck traveled back from Rikers Island, the weight of Jamal's predicament floating in the air. The sound of the car's engine provided a soundtrack that enveloped them. Justice finally broke the silence.

"A fucking DEA agent?" she cursed, as she held onto the steering wheel.

"Justice, calm down."

"No, you calm down. This is not what my life was supposed to be, Luck. Did Keisha set this whole thing up?"

"I told you Keisha was no good," Luck declared. "She lied to you, and you gave the order to get Ox killed."

Justice's grip tightened on the steering wheel, her knuckles turning white as she absorbed Luck's words. Lights blurred, mirroring her confused mind.

"I'm not blaming you, Justice," he continued. "But this is exactly the type of person Keisha is. She's a snake, and she needs her head cut off."

The words just hung in the confined space of the car, each syllable resonating with the complexities of their past and the path they found themselves on. Deception was no match for truth, as Justice faced the consequences of misplaced trust.

The car idled at the side of the road. "Justice," Luck began. He knew the words he was about to speak were capable of shattering the equilibrium they had maintained. "It's something I gotta ask you to do, and I know it's gonna be hard for you to accept this but... Jamal, he ain't built for this lifestyle. He's weak, the total opposite of you."

Justice betrayed a momentary emptiness as she processed the gravity of Luck's proposition. A smile, however, began to curve across her lips, the irony not lost on her.

"Fuck you, Luck," she replied, her eyes ablaze with a fire that matched the burning cityscape outside. The audacity of such a demand ignited anger inside of her. "You must be out of your mind if you think I'm going to kill my own brother. What the fuck is wrong with you?"

"This is the game, Justice. This is what comes with this shit. When you've been through what I been through, you see the world differently. Ain't no such thing as friends and family in this business. It's all about the money."

Justice turned away, her eyes on the cityscape beyond the window. "I'm not killing my brother. That's my blood. I'm not you. I didn't ask for this. And to tell you the truth, I don't even want it anymore. I want out, Luck."

"There is no out, Justice. This is it. And regardless if he's your brother or your father, you don't dictate what goes on in these streets," Luck explained. "Jamal... he should've never picked that gun up. You gotta understand... these streets ain't for everybody."

The words were a somber acknowledgment of a truth that refused to be ignored. In that car, the battle lines were drawn — between Justice's desire for a life beyond the streets and Luck's adherence to the ruthless laws of the streets.

In the loft, Justice sat on the edge of her bed, Luck's words playing on a mental loop like a glitched audio file. The city outside buzzed with life, but her mind was trapped on that phrase—*'these streets ain't for everybody.'* As the night unfolded, sleep eluded her, leaving her alone with the haunting shadows of guilt.

Justice tossed and turned, wrestling with the reality of the lifestyle that had swallowed her and her brother. She had tried to shield Jamal, but the streets had a magnetic pull, dragging him deeper into a world she wished he'd never entered.

Tears stained her pillow as the weight of responsibility settled on her shoulders. The guilt clawed at her insides, because in some twisted way, she had led Jamal down this path — it was her fault.

Rikers Island, where real killers thrived, was not the stage for a young man assigned a role by circumstance. This wasn't a script; it was a raw, unfiltered reality, and Justice knew Jamal wasn't built for it.

With her heart heavy with worry, Justice turned to prayer. In the quiet of the night, she begged for strength and safety for her brother in a dangerous place.

As morning light crept into the room, Justice wiped away the last of her tears and prepared herself for the challenges ahead. The focus in her mind was to extricate Jamal from the confines of Rikers Island. But to do that, she needed to confront the one person who could potentially facilitate his release — Bishop.

MDC - BROOKLYN, NEW YORK

In the Metropolitan Detention Center, the stench of misery and aggression lingered. Bishop's cell was a cramped den bearing the scars of territorial disputes, distant shouts and iron.

Bishop had transformed inside the confines of the MDC. His presence now commanded respect in the hierarchy of the facility. His name, both feared and reverenced, made noise through the tier, marking him as one of the grimiest and most notorious within the prison.

The C.O approached Bishop's cell. "Lindsey, you got a visit!" he shouted.

Bishop, rising from his makeshift throne, surveyed his domain with a gleam in his eyes. The air was thick with the odor of sweat from continuous workouts and latent aggression as he dressed himself in the uniform of the incarcerated — a uniform that held no allegiance but to the ruthless code of the streets.

Escorted through the corridors, Bishop's presence sent a ripple of tension through the inmates. In their eyes, he was a living legend, a symbol of the spirit that refused to be broken by the machinery of the system.

The visitation room offered a temporary sanctuary from the war-zone. Cold tables and chairs framed a space where moments of connection occurred amidst the isolation.

As Bishop took his seat behind the dividing glass, he wondered who was there to visit him.

The atmosphere in the visitation area was uneasy. The smell of institutional cleaners and hushed conversations filled the space. Justice, having successfully gone through the security protocols, passed through the doors, and stepped into the belly of the beast. The clang of the door shutting behind her seemed to mark an ominous passage.

Guided down a corridor by a corrections officer, each step carried her deeper into the belly. The long hallway stretched endlessly, and the visiting room was just ahead.

Separated by the divide of brick and glass, visitors and inmates coexisted in a space that blurred the lines between yearning and captivity. Following the directions of the corrections officer, Justice found herself at visitation table number 12.

The chair scraped against the cold floor as she pulled it out. On the other side of the partition, Bishop sat, his presence confined and restrained.

Bishop's eyes met Justice's. The glass distorted their connection, turning it into a dance between proximity and distance. The whispered conversations and sporadic clinks of metal merged into the soundtrack of the visitation room.

A deep breath steadied Justice as she confronted Bishop. The silence between them, heavy with unspoken truths and unresolved history, stretched like an invisible bridge. At that moment, the complexities of their relationship played out.

The cold receiver pressed against Justice's ear as she took a moment to collect herself. On the other side of the glass barrier, Bishop also performed the same action.

"Keisha lied about Ox, Bishop..." she told him. The truth, like a concealed weapon, was drawn into the open.

Bishop's facade cracked, and for a moment, the hard edges of his street-honed exterior softened. In the confined space where the scent of disinfectant lingered, Bishop's eyes, usually sharp and vigilant, betrayed a vulnerability. The concrete walls seemed to absorb the heaviness of what he had just heard, creating a somber backdrop.

He faced Justice from behind the glass and remained silent. His eyes hardened by the street life.

"Jamal told me everything," Justice continued, her voice trembling with anger and tears in her eyes. "How could you use my little brother like that, Bishop? I trusted you."

Bishop shook his head. "Misplaced trust is a one-way ticket to a grave." His voice slithered through the receiver. "Sometimes, the person you trust the most turns out to be the same motherfucka prayin' on your downfall."

Justice absorbed Bishop's words. In the streets where survival demanded ruthless choices, loyalty was a fragile currency, and it could be devalued in an instant.

"Jamal ain't built for these streets, and you know it, Bishop. You took advantage of him..." she cried.

Bishop let out a short, bitter laugh. "Half the niggas in here wasn't built to do the shit they did. It wasn't my responsibility to watch over that lil' nigga, that's on you. He said he wanted to put in work, so I gave him some work."

The words hung between them, a cold acknowledgment of the nature of the streets. Bishop's perspective offered no solace to Justice. In the jungle, survival was the objective, and he followed the unspoken rules.

Justice sniffled, her teary eyes fixed on Bishop as she wiped her face. "I need you to help me get Jamal out."

Bishop, standing abruptly, held onto the receiver. His response was cold. "I can't do that, Justice," he declared. "Only person I can help in this situation is myself." The receiver fell silent as Bishop hung up, leaving Justice in a state of bewilderment. "C.O!" he yelled, summoning the correctional officer to escort him away, leaving Justice with unanswered questions lingering in the air of the visitation room.

"Bishop!" she called out as he disappeared from view. The steel table, a witness to the abrupt end of their conversation, and Justice felt a surge of confusion and panic.

Was Bishop planning to snitch?

The thought clawed at her conscious. Faced with uncertainty, she recognized the urgency of time. Gathering herself, Justice left the visitation room. The chessboard had shifted once again, and she needed a new strategy to navigate the game that now threatened not only her brother's fate but their entire existence.

❧ 10 ❧

In the grimy streets of New York City, General Lee prowled through the fog. His sharp eyes scanned the alleys, searching for any trace of Justice. Derrick's debt, now inherited by Justice, was all Lee was thinking about, driving him to relentless pursuit.

Lee's network of informants had passed along tidbits of information about Justice's whereabouts. He knew the streets like the back of his hand, and every whisper in the concrete jungle became a clue leading him closer to his target.

As he delved deeper into the city, Lee became impatient. He needed to find Justice, settle the debt, and send a message to the streets that General Lee's business was not to be fucked with.

On Rikers, Jamal's time turned into a struggle for survival. Each day brought new challenges, and he found himself constantly looking over his shoulder, uncertain of the danger that lurked.

The predatory nature of the environment had forced Jamal to take a drastic step—seeking refuge in protective custody. The small cell offered him a momentary break from the constant threats and violence that flooded general population. However, safety came at the cost of isolation, and the walls that protected him also confined him to a lonely existence.

Nightime was the cruelest part of his routine. As the lights dimmed, he lay on his narrow bunk, surrounded by the distant conversations and the occasional clang of iron against iron. The weight of his circumstances felt like a one hundred pound dumbbell on his chest, and in the solitude of his cell, Jamal struggled with the reality of his choices.

The tears, once a rare expression of vulnerability, now flowed freely in the darkness. Each drop carried the weight of regret, fear, and the loneliness that accompanied his isolation. The sounds of his quiet sobs were drowned out by the consistent noise around him.

Jamal fought not only against the external threats but also the internal demons that clawed at his conscience. Protective custody offered a shield from physical harm, but it couldn't protect him from the haunting memories and knowing that what he had done led him to this bleak existence.

In the quiet sanctuary of her modest townhome, Keisha cradled her newborn daughter, enveloped in the soothing warmth of the nursery. Soft rays of sunlight filtered through the sheer curtains, splashing an energetic glow onto the scene, and the air was filled with a serene calmness.

Only six and a half months had passed since the birth of her daughter, Kiani, yet the weight of those months was heavy on Keisha's shoulders. As she stared into the innocent eyes of her delicate child, a flood of emotions surged inside of her. The room, painted in pastel hues and the tender lullabies playing softly in the background, provided some refuge from the drama that lurked beyond its walls.

Despite the tranquility, Keisha carried the burden of her choices. Betraying her own flesh and blood, especially her brother Luck, was a drastic measure she was willing to take for the promise of a better life. She understood the gravity of her actions, but in the quiet moments with her daughter, she sought normalcy and a glimpse of a future free from the shackles of her past.

"I love you, my precious child," Keisha whispered, her voice a tender caress in the hushed room. As she stared down at Kiani's innocent face, determination shone in her eyes. It was a silent promise to provide her daughter with a life untouched by the evils that haunted her own existence.

The room, filled with the fragrance of baby lotion and the soft coos of the infant, became a haven where Keisha envisioned a different reality. A reality free from fear and betrayal, where motherhood brings simple joy.

"Okay, so, let me get this straight," Agent Parker's voice sliced through Keisha's moment of contemplation, pulling her back to the reality of the situation. "You purchased the BMW, and two days later you gave the keys to who?" His penetrating eyes fixed on Keisha, dissecting her every word for inconsistencies.

Keisha squared her shoulders. "Justice Carter," she replied. "I gave the keys to the BMW to Justice. That's all I can tell you."

Agent Mills, Parker's partner, leaned forward, her eyes probing for any signs of deceit. "And you claim you don't know anything about the murder of DEA agent Eric Hayes?"

"A murder?" Keisha maintained her composure. "I don't know anything about a murder. I'm just a regular person trying to live a normal life with my child."

Parker and Mills exchanged skeptical glances as Keisha recounted the details of the BMW. Despite their doubts, they decided to follow up on the new lead—Justice Carter.

But before their departure, Agent Parker pulled a small, discreet recording/tracking device from his pocket. "We need you to make sure this gets into your brother's car," he instructed.

Keisha stared at the device in Agent Parker's outstretched hand. "Y'all tryna get me killed? Lucian's not stupid."

"Just do what we tell you to do, Miss Beckford," Agent Mills insisted.

The door closed behind the federal agents, leaving Keisha alone with her decision. She looked at the device in her hands, a small object that could change her life and the lives of those around her. Especially in relation to Justice, a friend she had known for the majority of her life. The memories of their history played back in her mind—laughter, secrets, and the bond that had weathered the storms of their past.

But, as Keisha sat alone with her newborn daughter, she realized the truth: friends didn't tread the paths she had chosen. The dangerous game she played remained unseen by those who believed they knew her best.

And Justice, in her world of loyalty and twisted morality, remained oblivious to what was brewing. Keisha's involvement in the federal investigation was spreading. Little did Justice know, the stakes were about to escalate and alter their friendship.

ONE WEEK LATER

As Luck sat in his plush Mercedes Benz, the city's pulse throbbed around him. His mind, a battlefield of conflicting interests, wrestled with the dissonance of his actions. Jamal's situation with the cartel hung in the air like a storm cloud. The cartel's pressure to spill blood was strong, and Luck wrestled with the dilemma of sacrificing a young life for survival.

Deep down, he knew Jamal wasn't cut out for the streets. The internal struggle mirrored the external threats encircling him. The cartel's demands went against Luck's own morals, but in the world he navigated, sentimentality was a luxury he couldn't afford.

As for his sister, Keisha, she added another layer of complexity. An instinctual unease simmered beneath the surface. Luck had always trusted his instincts, and they whispered warnings about Keisha's hidden agenda. The need to neutralize her, to maintain control over the balance he had crafted, became a pressing concern. Trust was rare, and family bonds were as much a liability as an asset.

Justice's Benz pulled up on the side of Luck's and the passenger window came down. "What's so important?" She asked.

"Get in. We need to talk," Luck replied.

Justice eyed Luck from the driver's side of her Mercedes.

The tension between them was thick. She hesitated for a moment, contemplating the risks of getting entangled deeper into Luck's turbulent world. Nevertheless, a sense of responsibility and the urgency of the situation propelled her to slide into the luxurious leather seat beside him.

The vehicles now formed a meeting ground, sheltered from the prying eyes of the city. Inside the confined space, the ambiance mirrored the strained relationship between Justice and Luck. The idling engine's low hum highlighted the seriousness of the issues.

Luck, staring straight ahead, finally broke the silence. "We got some serious shit to discuss, Justice. Things are getting out of control."

Justice leaned forward. "What's the problem?"

"The cartel is breathing down my neck. They want Jamal's blood. And on top of that, I still got that problem with Keisha."

Justice's eyes narrowed at the mention of her brother. "No one's touching Jamal. And what about Keisha?"

Luck leaned back, rubbing his temples as if trying to alleviate a persistent headache. "I asked you to handle her, Justice. But you haven't taken care of it."

"I'm not a killer, Luck. And I won't take part in whatever twisted plan you got. Let me ask you something..." Justice looked directly into Luck's eyes. "Did you know that was a DEA agent?"

Despite his reluctance, Luck realized that revealing the truth would jeopardize countless lives. He looked away from her. "Nah. I had no idea," he told her.

Justice studied his face, searching for any hint of deception. The weight of the truth hung between them, a truth too dangerous to be spoken aloud. In the confines of the Mercedes, shadows danced across Luck's features, obscuring the turmoil beneath the surface.

"You swear?" Justice pressed.

Luck, avoiding direct eye contact, nodded. "I swear, Justice. I would never have let you go down there if I knew."

The air inside the car seemed charged with tension.

"But now that they're involved, we gotta figure out a way to handle it," Luck continued, breaking the uneasy silence. "And Keisha—"

Justice interrupted him. "I'm not killing Keisha, Luck."

"Not even if I paid you a million dollars?" Luck proposed.

Justice's mind raced through the possibilities. A million dollars could be the ticket to a new life, far from the streets. The security for her and Jamal tugged at her conscious, creating a moment of contemplation.

As she weighed the offer, a myriad of images flashed through Justice's mind — memories of the struggles they faced, the bonds of friendship that had endured, and the truth that the life they led was a relentless force.

Finally, Justice shook her head. "No amount of money can change what's happened, Luck. I won't turn against my friend, no matter the price."

Luck had hoped the thought of financial freedom would sway Justice, but her commitment to her friend remained intact.

"Alright, Justice," he conceded. "But remember, this path we're on, it's gonna get darker. And we might not all make it out."

72 HOURS LATER

The cold walls of Rikers Island enclosed Jamal as he sat across from federal agents, Parker and Mills. The agents wasted no time diving into the interrogation. Seasoned in the art of extracting information, they pressed him, seeking any crack in his defense. The walls seemed to close in as questions intensified, each one a calculated attempt to force Jamal into divulging crucial information.

Despite the pressure, Jamal stuck to the code of the streets, refusing to betray the unspoken rules that governed his world. "I don't know anything about a murder, man. I was just caught up in some other shit," he asserted, his voice edged with frustration.

Mills joined the conversation. "We've got evidence linking the gun found in your possession to the crime scene. You better start talking."

But Jamal held firm and kept his silence.

However, the agents escalated their tactics. They insinuated that cooperation could lead to a more lenient sentence, an offer Jamal quickly dismissed. The dance went on, and the game unfolded in the interrogation room.

Then, the moment arrived. The agents, perhaps sensing the need to change their strategy, played a recording. It was a carefully crafted snippet of a conversation between Luck and Justice discussing the potential of Jamal's demise. The tape, edited strategically, painted a damning picture.

As Jamal listened, a mix of emotions washed over his face—betrayal, shock, and the realization that his sister might be involved in a plot against him.

"You hear that, Jamal?" Agent Mills challenged. "Your own

sister is talking about putting you down. You gonna protect them, even after this?"

Jamal felt the ground shift beneath him. The code he held dear now collided with the reality that loyalty might be a one-way street. Caught in the crossfire of family ties and the life-style, Jamal found himself at a pivotal juncture, a decision lingering that could alter the course of his fate.

THE PROFFER

The cold room in the federal building set the stage for Bishop's cooperation with agents Mills and Parker. Bishop, once feared on the streets, now faced a crossroads.

"I'll tell you everything," Bishop began. He told them about the unsolved murders in New York, providing intricate details that only someone deeply entrenched in the underworld could possess. Each revelation painted a vivid picture of the darkness beneath the city's surface.

Seated across the table from federal agents, the tape recorder whirring between them, Bishop navigated the questions with a careful dance. Every word, each admission, was documented for the record. The proffer agreement loomed over the room, a shadow that Bishop couldn't escape.

"And then there's the one in Virginia," Bishop continued, his eyes distant as he recounted the events leading to the murder, the players involved, and the motives that fueled the tragedy. The room felt heavy with his words.

The agents, well-versed in the art of turning witnesses, probed Bishop for details about Luck and the criminal enter-prise that had gripped the city. Bishop, fully aware of the consequences, chose to cooperate, opting for a chance at leniency rather than a lifetime behind bars.

As he recounted the workings of Luck's empire, he couldn't shake the echoes of his former life—the streets that once obeyed his commands and the loyalty that now seemed like a distant memory. The room, flooded in fluorescent lights, witnessed the unraveling of alliances, the collateral damage of the streets.

Each disclosure pushed Bishop farther from his long-held code. The decision to turn states evidence marked a shift, a betrayal that vibrated through the streets of New York.

Agent Parker, pen scratching across the notepad, listened intently, probing for every piece of information that could lead to an arrest. As Bishop approached the truth, the room grew tense with the secret he had kept for someone else.

"So, what about Ox?" Agent Parker questioned.

Bishop took a deep breath, wiping his face with both hands. The silence lingered before he uttered the words that would shift the course of the investigation. "I did that," he confessed.

Agent Parker's eyebrows furrowed in surprise. "You killed Ox? But, weren't you guys friends?"

"Betrayal is a debt paid in lead. When a friend turns Judas, the trigger becomes the only judge and jury."

"Ox was a Judas?" Agent Mills asked.

Bishop leaned forward, elbows on the table, his eyes fixed on a point in the middle distance as he began to unravel the tangled threads of betrayal. "I was told the word came down from Luck that Ox was no good," Bishop admitted. "Apparently, Keisha lied and sent word through Justice," he continued.

He glanced towards the mirrored glass that concealed the unseen observers. "Justice, she told me to handle it," he concluded, the words heavy with the acknowledgment of a choice made in the dark. The room, now charged with the truth, bore witness to the dance of power, lies, and survival that dictated the fates of those caught up in the city's grasp.

"So, you killed Ox for nothing?" Agent Parker's question hung there. The room seemed to hold its breath, anticipating Bishop's response, his justification for a murder that now appeared senseless.

His eyes, windows to a soul burdened by the streets, held a glint of remorse. "It wasn't for nothing," he replied. "It was an order. If I didn't do it, it would've been me…"

The clanging of cell doors vibrated through the narrow passageways of Rikers Island, the abrasive sound signaling an interruption in the prison's monotonous rhythm. A harsh voice shattered the oppressive silence.

"Carter! You got a visit!"

Jamal's ears caught the announcement, and a surge of emotions flowed through him. It had been nearly a week since Justice's last visit, and the playback of the federal agents' recording echoed in his mind like a haunting refrain. His decision was made. As soon as Justice showed her face, he intended to confront her, to unravel the truth that had been concealed from him.

The cold ambiance of the prison intensified as Jamal emerged from the shadows of his cell. Dim flickering lights cast long, distorted shadows as he moved through the corridors.

Being that Jamal's case was high profile, his visitation privileges set him apart from the general prison population.

Entering the visitation area, he felt the weight of the moment in the air.

As he made his way toward the designated space, a series of iron bars and glass dividers framed the encounter. His eyes, filled with anger and confusion, met Justice's across the barrier. The exchange, charged with unspoken tension, unfolded within the confines of the visitation area.

"My life's only worth a million dollars?" Jamal opened the conversation, his words cutting through the air of the visitation room.

Justice, taken aback and confused, responded with a hesitant, "Huh?"

"The feds played me the tape, Justice," Jamal continued.

"What tape, Jamal? What are you talking about?"

"The tape where you and Luck are talking about killing me. That tape. How could you do some shit like this to me, Justice? We're family!" The accusation hung between them, a jagged edge cutting into the core of their bond.

A million dollars? Killing? Luck? It all clicked for Justice now. The feds must have tapped Luck's car. The pieces fell into place, revealing the game at play.

"It's a lie, Jamal. The feds are playing a dangerous game. That's not what was said in that conversation," she protested desperately, her voice cracking with the weight of emotions.

"I heard it, Justice! It was your voice!"

"Jamal, you gotta believe me. The feds are manipulating this."

The tension in the room escalated. "I'm turning states evidence. Fuck that. I don't trust none of you motherfuckas..."

"No, Jamal... please don't do that," Justice pleaded, her voice cracking with desperation. Her eyes locked onto her brother's, hoping to bridge the growing chasm between them.

The walls of the visitation room seemed to close in, amplifying the weight of the moment. Time was suspended as the siblings struggled with the reality that now threatened to sever the ties that bound them.

"Jamal, you know me. You know us. We're not capable of what they're accusing us of," Justice implored. The connection that had weathered countless storms now teetered on the brink, and she fought to salvage the remnants of trust.

But Jamal, haunted by the recording and the betrayal, stood on his word. His eyes, once a reflection of family love, now held a distrust. The tape told a story of betrayal, and unraveling the lies felt impossible.

"I can't go down for something I didn't do, Justice," Jamal replied.

Justice extended her hand as if reaching across an unbridgeable divide. "Jamal, please. We need each other now more than ever. Don't let them tear us apart." Her plea hung in the air, a desperate hope that the ties of blood could withstand the tempest of external forces.

Justice's eyes reddened from tears as she prepared to unravel the painful truth that had driven a wedge between her and her brother. She took a deep breath, searching for the right words to mend the fractures that had emerged between them.

"Jamal," she began. "I need you to understand, to see why I did what I did. It's not an excuse, but it's the only way I can make you understand."

She described the journey into Luck's world and the desperate choices made. The room became a confessional, a space where truths, however painful, sought refuge.

"I got involved with Luck because I thought I could change things for us, for you," she admitted, her eyes never leaving Jamal's. "The debts, the struggles... I wanted to give you a chance, a future, without constantly looking over our shoulders. But I got in too deep, and the choices became a trap."

Tears glistened in Justice's eyes as she continued, "I did it for you, Jamal. For the barbershop, for a chance at a life free from this darkness. I wanted to honor Dad's memory, to provide for you the way he would have wanted. But I lost sight of the path, Jamal. I let the money and the promise of a better life blind me to the consequences. I never meant for things to spiral out of control like this."

She reached out, her hand trembling as she rested it against the cold glass that separated them. "Dad wouldn't have wanted this for us," she whispered. "He would've told us to stand strong, to face the hardships together, not to get lost in a world that would tear us apart."

As Justice spoke, she peeled back the layers of her decisions, exposing the vulnerability that lay beneath. "I secured the barbershop, Jamal," she confessed, a smidgen of hope in her eyes. "I've been fixing it up, making it a place where you can stand tall and proud, away from the bullshit that has haunted us."

A thick silence settled between them as Jamal absorbed the weight of his sister's words.

"Don't turn state's evidence, Jamal, please," she begged, her eyes pleading for mercy. "Luck will see that as a betrayal, and he won't hesitate to come after you. I've seen what he's capable of. I can't lose you, too."

Their father's memory seemed to linger in the room, urging them to find a way back to each other. Justice, her voice now a tender plea, said, "We can get through this dark place with each other, Jamal. We're family, and family sticks together, no matter how tough it gets. Please, don't let them do this to us."

Jamal stared at Justice, his eyes reflecting an array of emotions. Tears welled, mirroring the conflict inside of him. He wanted desperately to believe her, to hold on to the lifeline she was offering, but a nagging doubt was evident. Jamal's intuition hinted that she could be a deceptive player in this dangerous game.

"Yeah, everything you said sounds good," Jamal told her, a bitter taste lingering on his tongue, "but the reality is that I'm stuck in this hell, fighting for my life against the devil." Jamal turned on his heels without uttering another word, and walked away from the small visitation area, leaving Justice alone in the silence of the room.

❧ 11 ❧

Justice stepped through the glass doors of the FBI building, her heart pounding in her chest. The air inside seemed to stifle her as she approached the security checkpoint. All she could think about was Jamal.

The security personnel, stern-faced and efficient, scrutinized her identification before granting her passage. She sensed the burden of her forthcoming confession, the seriousness of exposing her criminal activities.

Walking through the corridors, Justice couldn't escape the sense that every glance from the passing pedestrians bore into her, dissecting her secrets. She made her way to the designated room where federal agents awaited her testimony.

Bright lights in the cold room intensified the seriousness. Seated around a table were stern-faced agents, their expressions, an indication of the gravity of the information they sought. Agent Parker, the one who had interrogated Bishop, looked up as Justice entered.

"Take a seat, Ms. Carter," Agent Parker instructed, his tone formal and businesslike.

Justice complied, the chair feeling uncomfortably rigid beneath her. As she began to recount the details of her involvement in various murders, she noticed the agents exchanging glances. She couldn't escape the sensation that she was digging her own grave.

Agent Parker, pen in hand, transcribed her words meticulously. Silent judgments and heavy crimes filled the room. Justice's narrative unfolded - betrayal, deception, and violence spun over the course of her descent into the criminal underworld.

Suddenly, a federal agent approached, his demeanor was stern. He placed cold handcuffs on the table before her, the sound of metal vibrating in the room.

Justice's eyes widened.

"Ms. Carter, you are under arrest for your involvement in these crimes. Anything you say can and will be used against you in a court of law," the agent said with practiced authority.

In the blink of an eye, the scene shifted. The FBI room dissolved, replaced by the warm hues of Justice's loft. She sat upright in bed, her heart racing, beads of sweat clinging to her forehead. The handcuffs were gone, replaced by the comforting touch of her bed sheets.

Justice took a moment to collect herself, the weight of the dream still haunting her waking hours. The loft was quiet, the only sound was the faint noises from outside. She couldn't shake the feeling that the boundary between dreams and the reality she had willingly entered was growing thin.

She sat on the edge of her bed. The loft, with exposed brick walls and remnants of her past, felt both comforting and haunting. Her eyes wandered, settling on a family photo—a reminder of strained bonds caused by her choices.

A heavy sigh escaped her lips as she contemplated her actions. The faces of those she had harmed, the lives she had disrupted, danced before her eyes. The weight of guilt settled on her shoulders, a burden she could no longer ignore. The vividness of the nightmare had forced her to confront the consequences of her choices, and the line between right and wrong blurred in the harsh light of self-reflection.

Justice's hands trembled as she reached for a glass of water on the nightstand. The cool liquid did little to soothe the questions that burned inside of her. *Was her destiny to redeem herself and protect her loved ones?*

The space of the loft seemed to shrink around her. Her mind raced with possibilities, each step she had taken flashing before her like a series of warnings. It was time to make a decision, to redefine the course of her life.

As she contemplated her next steps, it dawned on her—a catalyst born from the nightmarish revelation. She couldn't outrun the consequences of her actions, but she could control the path that lay ahead. A new desire fueled her contemplation—she would protect herself and, above all, her family.

She glanced at the clock ticking away on the wall. The city outside her loft window buzzed with its own rhythm—a rhythm that seemed to synchronize with the beating of her conflicted heart. To redeem herself and find a new future, Justice had to break free from the shackles of the criminal world.

She knew that saving Jamal was her top priority. As she drove through the streets, her mind raced with thoughts of the deadly path she was about to embark on. The city's shadows seemed to close in around her, mirroring the darkness she was determined to escape.

Her first destination was the FBI field office. The imposing building loomed ahead, a symbol of both authority and, now, potential salvation. Justice took a deep breath, steadying herself before entering.

"I need to speak to someone about the criminal organization known as 'Luck's Crew,'" Justice stated.

The receptionist eyed her skeptically, but Justice didn't budge. Before long, she found herself in a room with Agent Parker, the very agent who had interrogated Bishop.

"Start talking," Agent Parker demanded.

Justice unraveled the web of criminal activities orchestrated by Luck and his crew. She detailed their operations, alliances, and the extent of her involvement. As she spoke, a weight lifted off her shoulders, replaced by the weight of responsibility.

"I can help you bring them down, but I need something in return," Justice asserted, her eyes locking onto Agent Parker's.

He raised an eyebrow, prompting her to continue.

"Promise me you'll protect my brother, Jamal. He's innocent in all of this. If I'm going to risk everything to help you, I need your assurance that he'll be safe."

Agent Parker leaned back, considering her plea. The room hung in tense silence until he finally nodded.

"We can arrange witness protection for Jamal. But you have to deliver on your end. We'll be watching, Justice."

And so, Justice's journey for redemption began. The alliance with law enforcement became a delicate dance, with each step carrying the weight of her consequences. While informing the FBI, she couldn't shake the feeling of being watched by the authorities and her own past.

The sound of gunfire splashed through the night as agents stormed the cathedral. They moved with precision, weapons drawn, adrenaline pumping. Their footsteps were drowned out by the shouted orders and the clatter of kicked-open doors.

Luck's crew, caught off guard, responded with a hail of bullets. The air became suffused with the scent of gunpowder. In the corridors, shadows danced with the muzzle flashes. Agent Parker, leading the charge, pressed forward, determination all over his face.

"Federal agents! Drop your weapons!" he bellowed, his voice cutting through the mayhem.

But Luck's crew fought back, defending their turf. Bullets flew past, finding their marks or embedding themselves into the cathedral's ancient stone. The sharp reports of gunfire whizzing through the cavernous space.

Luck, alerted to the raid, had vanished into the maze like passages beneath the cathedral. The agents, unaware of his escape, pushed on, determined to dismantle the criminal network. But Luck was already plotting his next move, leaving behind a trail of confusion and thwarted justice.

As the intensity of the firefight escalated, the cathedral's stained glass windows shattered, casting kaleidoscopic patterns on the blood-stained floor. The battle raged on until the last of the gunfire subsided, leaving behind a silent, smoke-filled battleground.

In the aftermath, wounded agents tended to their injuries, and the smoke slowly cleared, revealing the cathedral's scars. The hunt for Luck had intensified, and the city braced itself for what was coming.

The night air was heavy with secrets as Justice and Luck met in a secluded area of Tryon, a sleepy town in rural North Carolina. The town, nestled between rolling hills and surrounded by dense forests, exuded an eerie tranquility under the moonlit sky.

Luck's Mercedes idled in the alley, its polished surface reflecting the glow of the streetlights. The air, crisp and scented with pine, carried the distant sound of an owl's hoot.

Once inside the car, Luck stared into Justice's eyes She was the one person he believed hadn't turned against him. The engine roared to life, drowning out the nocturnal sounds that accompanied their secret meeting.

The highway stretched ahead, a ribbon of asphalt cutting through the heart of Tyron. The few scattered houses along the roadside slept in blissful ignorance of the coming drama. The lights from the town's only diner painted a picturesque glow on the deserted streets.

Luck spoke. "Justice, you're all I got left. Everyone else has betrayed me, but not you, right?"

Justice nodded, playing the role she had always known. "Of course, Luck. You know I got your back."

As they merged onto the highway, the conversation flowed like a river of confessions. Luck, unburdening his soul, spoke on everything; the betrayals, the alliances that shattered like glass, he spoke of the empire he had built, which was now crumbling around him, and he discussed the federal agents who seemed to know his every move.

The miles passed, and with each one, the tension in the car thickened. The quaint charm of Tyron faded into the rearview mirror as they continued their journey through the winding roads of the Carolina night.

In a moment of vulnerability, Luck veered off the highway and parked in a motel lot outside Tyron. The neon sign of the "Whispering Pines Motel" was illuminated as they entered the room.

The air in the motel room was filled with a mix of nostalgia and doom. The light from the neon sign outside cast shadows on the walls, bearing witness to the secrets shared between Justice and Luck.

Sitting on the edge of the worn motel bed, the gravity of Luck's words lingered. Little did he know, the trap had been set, and the net was closing in.

The light in the small motel room created an intimate atmosphere. Justice, sensing the gravity of the situation, decided to keep Luck at ease. She sat close to him on the edge of the bed. She began to talk, sharing stories of their past. As their conversation deepened, she found herself gently running her hand over Luck's waves, a touch filled with a mix of familiarity and comfort.

Justice's movements were subtle but deliberate, creating a sense of closeness. In the glow of the bedside lamp, their conversation took on an intimate quality, designed to distract Luck from the coming danger. The shadows danced on the walls, hiding the complexities of the situation, and for a brief moment, they were just two people seeking each other's company.

Justice's phone vibrated on the nightstand. She glanced at the message from Agent Parker, a silent cue that the FBI was closing in.

Luck, already on edge, eyed Justice with suspicion. The

room, once an intimate haven, now transformed into a space of conflicting motives.

In the darkness, they each reached for their concealed weapons simultaneously. Luck's eyes focused on Justice's.

"What the fuck is this, Justice? You turnin' on me too?"

"I'm not turning on you, Luck. I'm saving you from yourself," Justice responded.

Before a trigger was pulled, the door exploded inward, splinters of wood scattering like shrapnel. Federal agents stormed in, guns drawn, shouting commands.

"Drop your weapons! You're under arrest!" Agent Parker shouted.

The room became a blur of flashing lights, muffled shouts, and the clatter of firearms hitting the floor.

"You think this gon' change anything, Justice? I'ma remember this!" Luck shouted.

"You should've listened, Luck," Justice replied.

In the blink of an eye, Luck was surrounded, outgunned and outnumbered. Justice, caught between the loyalty she had to the streets and her brother's freedom, dropped her weapon.

"You made the right choice. Now, let's clean up this mess," Agent Parker said to Justice.

The net had finally closed, leaving behind broken dreams, and the remnants of a life unraveled.

❧ 12 ❧

The courtroom, covered in bright overhead lights, throbbed with anticipation. Wooden benches, occupied by a mix of spectators, journalists, and law enforcement, lined the periphery.

At the front, the judge's bench towered over the courtroom. The judge, a stern figure in black robes, surveyed the room.

Judge Harlan Whitman, a figure of authority with a reputation for fair but firm rulings, presided over the courtroom. His graying hair and penetrating eyes bespoke years of experience, and his measured voice commanded attention as he addressed the room. The attorneys on both sides knew that before them sat a jurist with a commitment to justice.

Facing each other across the well-worn oak floor were the legal adversaries. The prosecution, a team of determined attorneys armed with stacks of evidence, occupied one side.

The lead prosecutor; Sarah Rodriguez was a seasoned attorney known for her sharp intellect and relentless pursuit of justice. Sarah had an impressive track record of convictions in high-profile cases.

The assistant prosecutors were Michael Turner and Karen Chang. Michael, a brilliant legal mind, often focused on building airtight cases, while Karen, equally formidable, had a reputation for dissecting the defense's arguments with surgical precision.

On the other side, the defense, clad in tailored suits, exuded confidence and apprehension.

Lead defense attorney Julius "JT" Thompson was a veteran defense attorney with a knack for turning the tide in favor of his clients. JT, as his colleagues called him, had a reputation for his charismatic courtroom presence and his ability to sow reasonable doubt.

His defense co-counsel comprised Emily Stevens, a rising star in the defense world who brought a fresh perspective, and Marcus Harris, who has a background in criminal psychology, and often provided insights that shaped their defense strategy.

In the defendant's section, Luck and his crew sat side by side. The weight of the charges against them showed in the set of their jaws and the furrow of their brows. As the clerk called the court to order, the room fell into a silence. With the trial underway, the fate of those involved hung in the balance.

Lead Prosecutor Sarah Rodriguez strides to the front, her eyes scanning the jury.

"Good morning, ladies and gentlemen of the jury. Today, we will expose a web of criminal activities orchestrated by the defendants—Lucian "Luck" Beckford and his crew. The charges include racketeering, drug trafficking, and, most notably, a series of violent murders."

She outlined the prosecution's case, emphasizing evidence

and witness testimonies that will establish guilt beyond a reasonable doubt.

Lead Defense Attorney Julius Thompson stepped forward, exuding charm.

"Ladies and gentlemen, not everything is as it seems. We're not denying that our clients have led colorful lives, but the prosecution will struggle to prove their direct involvement in these alleged crimes. Keep an open mind, and you'll find that there's more to this story than meets the eye."

Thompson hinted at the unreliability of witnesses and challenges the credibility of the evidence presented.

The first to take the stand was Keisha Beckford, Luck's biological sister. Dressed in a somber suit, she hesitated before speaking.

"Ms. Beckford, can you describe your relationship with the defendant, Lucian "Luck" Bedford?" Attorney Rodriguez questioned.

"He's my brother," Keisha answered. "but he also pulled me into this life. He was the one who showed me the ropes, introduced me to the streets."

"Can you describe the extent of your brother's involvement in your entry into the criminal world?"

"He... he said it was the only way to survive. That I didn't have a choice..."

"So, your loyalty to him could be clouded by family ties. How do we know you're not trying to protect yourself by throwing your brother under the bus?" Defense Attorney Thompson asked.

"I'm not..." Keisha answered.

Bishop, with a composed demeanor, followed. His testimony unraveled the inner workings of the criminal organization, but the defense aimed to cast doubt.

"Mr. Lindsey, do you go by a name other than the one you were given at birth?" Attorney Rodriguez asked.

"Yes."

"What is that name?"

"Bishop..."

Attorney Rodriguez looked towards the jury, and then back to Bishop. "Bishop, was Luck involved in violent activities? Did he order murders?"

"Yes, but I—"

"So, you're saying Luck was the mastermind, and you were just following orders? Sounds like a convenient narrative to save your own skin." Defense attorney Thompson suggested.

The courtroom got quiet as Justice Carter, the star witness, stepped onto the witness stand. She prepared to reveal the web of crime she had been entangled in. Prosecution Attorney Rodriguez started the questioning.

"Ms. Carter, could you please recount the events leading to the murder of the DEA agent Eric Hayes in Virginia?"

Justice's eyes showed remorse. "It started with Luck's order. He had his sister, Keisha, provide me with a vehicle and told me it was thirty bricks of cocaine in the car. They instructed me to drop off the drugs and collect two bags of money, but when I got there, the two guys there tried to rob me, so I shot them..."

In the courtroom, pictures depicted the night of the murders - blood, bullet-holes, and the chilling aftermath.

"Objection, Your Honor." Defense attorney Thompson interrupted. "This is emotional manipulation."

Judge Whitman interjected. "Sustained. Stick to the facts, Counsel."

Prosecution steered the questioning to the murder of Justice's father's business partner. "Tell us about the barbershop, Ms. Carter."

Justice's voice quivered as she recounted the tragedy, providing a window into her conflicted allegiance.

The defense, known for their sharp strategies, approached Justice with a calculated intensity. "Ms. Carter, isn't it true that you had personal motivations for testifying against Luck? Perhaps to keep your brother free?"

"No. I mean, yes, but I want to make amends for the choices I've made. I can't carry this burden any longer."

"Ms. Carter, let's address the murder of Ox. Can you provide details on who was responsible for that crime?" Prosecution attorney Rodriguez asked.

Justice hesitated. She took a deep breath, her composure slipping. "It was... it was my brother, Jamal. He pulled the trigger, but..."

The truth was out. Silence filled the courtroom. Gasps and murmurs spread like wildfire among the spectators. The prosecution pressed further, sensing there was more to the story.

"Your brother, Jamal Carter, killed Ox. Can you explain why?"

Tears filled Justice's eyes as she unraveled the truth. "Keisha told me that Luck said Ox had to go, said he was a thief. I had ordered Bishop to do it, but he was too scared. Jamal got caught up in all of this, and I... I didn't know he would..."

The revelation left the jury and onlookers struggling with the realities of a world consumed by crime.

Defense attorney Mitchell stepped up. "Your Honor, we request that the testimony regarding Jamal Carter's involvement be struck from the record. It's prejudicial and irrelevant to the charges against Luck and his crew."

Attorney Rodriguez rebutted. "Your Honor, the connection is crucial to establishing the depth of the criminal network and Luck's influence. We urge the court to allow the testimony."

The courtroom buzzed and judge Whitman weighed the arguments.

"I'll allow the testimony, but the jury will be instructed to consider it only in relation to the broader criminal organization charges."

The legal maneuvering continued, each side trying to gain an upper hand. Objections and counter-objections created an atmosphere of constant anticipation. Unexpected revelations emerged, catching both legal teams off guard, and the drama unfolded as the trial delved deeper into Luck's criminal enterprise.

In the silent courtroom, the prosecution and defense teams prepared for their closing arguments. Attorney Rodriguez addressed the jury with a compelling narrative that sought to weave together the threads of betrayal and criminal conspiracy.

"Ladies and gentlemen of the jury, what you've heard paints a vivid picture of a criminal enterprise, masterminded by the defendant, Lucian Luck Carter. This is not just a story of illicit gains; it's a story of broken families, manipulated allegiances, and lives forever altered by the choices of one man."

As Rodriguez spoke, she connected the dots, creating a mosaic of guilt around Luck and his crew. The tension in the courtroom escalated, each word carrying the weight of the lives affected by the accused.

Attorney Thompson, leading the defense, presented a counter-narrative from the other side. Thompson's closing argument aimed to sow seeds of doubt, questioning the reliability of witnesses and challenging the prosecution's version of events.

"Ladies and gentlemen, my client is not a puppet master pulling the strings. He's a brother, a son, caught in a web spun by circumstances. What we've heard are stories, but stories can be twisted and turned to fit a particular narrative. The burden of proof rests on the prosecution, and reasonable doubt should guide your deliberations."

As Thompson crafted his argument, he painted Luck as a victim of circumstance, a man entangled in a world he couldn't control. In order to cast doubt on the prosecution's case, the defense had a clear strategy - humanize Luck.

Filled with anticipation, the courtroom witnessed the unfolding of the closing arguments, leaving the jury to deliberate on the scales of guilt and innocence.

The jury filed out, disappearing behind the closed doors to deliberate Lucian "Luck" Beckford's fate. Three days of tense waiting felt like an eternity for everyone involved—the prosecution, the defense, Luck and his crew, and the families of those affected.

In the secluded jury room, discussions grew heated. Voices rose and fell, each juror advocating for their interpretation of the evidence. Some leaned towards mercy, while others clung to the conviction that Luck and his crew were architects of their own demise.

"The evidence is damning, but is it enough to ruin these lives forever?" Juror #1 asked.

Juror #5 stood up from his seat. "We have a duty to society, to ensure that those who break the law face consequences."

They wrestled with the deliberations. Hours stretched into

days, and as the sun dipped below the horizon on the third day, the jury reached a verdict.

Back in the courtroom, the audience held its breath as the judge presided over the imminent revelation.

"Ladies and gentlemen of the jury, have you reached a verdict?" Judge Whitman asked.

The foreperson, a middle-aged woman with furrowed brows, nodded. She handed the folded slip of paper to the court clerk, who then passed it to Judge Whitman.

"Members of the jury, please stand and state your verdict," he told them.

"In the case of the United States versus Lucian "Luck" Beckford and others, we find the defendants..."

A pause settled in the courtroom.

"Guilty."

The room erupted; gasps, sobs, and stifled exclamations. Luck's tough demeanor was shattered as he realized the decision. His eyes shifted from the foreperson to the jury, seeking any hint of mercy.

"This shit ain't right!" Luck cursed. "Y'all don't know the whole story!"

Attempting to restore order as madness engulfed the room, the judge's gavel sounded. Exchanging glances of disbelief, the stunned and defeated defense team tried to process what had just happened.

The aftermath of the guilty verdict filled the air. As the judge's gavel struck the last note, sealing Luck and his crew's fate, a gasp swept through the room. Luck and his associates now stood vulnerable, handcuffed and escorted away by stern-faced federal agents.

Outside the courthouse, the media frenzy reached a fever

pitch, capturing the occasion with flashing cameras and probing questions. Headlines would soon chronicle the downfall of a criminal empire that had long plagued the city. The public, hungry for justice, absorbed the news with a mix of satisfaction and trepidation.

In the trial's aftermath, Jamal faced a different fate than he feared. Because he cooperated with federal authorities and Justice provided pivotal testimony, they dropped the murder charges related to the DEA agent. Instead, he was charged with manslaughter for his role in Ox's death.

While the consequences were severe, Jamal escaped a potential life sentence. The federal court sentenced him to a sixty-month term, acknowledging his willingness to help dismantle the criminal network. As Jamal began his prison sentence, he couldn't dodge the reality of his actions, but the reduced sentence offered some hope for redemption.

This turn of events left Justice with conflicting emotions. She had played a crucial role in securing a lighter sentence for her brother, but the guilt of putting him in such a predicament lingered. As Jamal entered prison, the siblings faced an uncertain future, each carrying the weight of their choices.

Transitioning from Rikers Island to the federal penitentiary proved to be a challenging shift for Jamal. The dynamics within federal prisons were distinct, with a heightened intensity and a unique set of rules. In this new environment, survival depended on navigating prison politics.

Jamal faced immediate adversity because of his status as a "hot" inmate—a label earned for cooperating with authorities. The federal prison system shunned those perceived as snitches, and Jamal found himself at the center of this dynamic.

Life behind bars was rough for Jamal. Threats, both overt and covert, appeared from every corner. The price of betrayals can range from a $20 bet to life itself. To adapt and survive, Jamal had to navigate these alliances and rivalries, always watching his back as he served his sentence in this unpredictable environment.

Unlike Jamal, a different set of circumstances marked Luck's entrance into the federal prison system. As a notorious kingpin, Luck arrived with an established reputation that commanded respect among his fellow inmates. The courts, perhaps, had chosen one of the most notorious federal penitentiaries for Luck's incarceration.

Luck's time in federal prison unfolded as a series of high-stakes maneuvers. Within the first year alone, he navigated through two attempts on his life, showcasing his ability to adapt to the dangerous games being played behind prison walls. Far from crumbling under the pressures of incarceration, Luck fit in and maintained his influence.

Prison life did little to change Luck's character. Within months, he had orchestrated a loyal crew within the prison confines, individuals willing to lie down their lives for him at a moment's notice. As he continued to wield influence and command respect, the federal penitentiary became another realm where his strategic mind and street-smart instincts played out, albeit in a different arena.

Luck's reputation had granted him access to certain privileges, but within these walls, even the most powerful had to move with caution.

In a corner, away from the prying eyes of surveillance cameras, Luck met with Officer Daniels, a corrections officer enticed by the allure of easy money.

"Officer Daniels, you know how it go. I need something to make life in here a bit more bearable," Luck said, his voice an inaudible murmur.

Daniels shifted, glancing around to make sure no one was watching. "You're playing with fire, Beckford. This ain't no game."

"It's only a game if you get caught. We both know the rules, Officer. You look out for me, and I'll make sure you are well taken care of."

The corrections officer hesitated, beads of sweat gathering on his forehead. He nodded. "I can get you what you need, but it'll cost you."

Luck smiled, revealing a glimpse of the street-smart charisma that had carried him this far. "Money talks, Officer. Consider it an investment in our continued understanding."

As he watched the officer walk away, Luck knew he had just secured a lifeline. The contraband would flow, and his influence would continue to extend its reach, even in the most unlikely places.

The chapel in the federal penitentiary echoed with the sound of chains and the shuffling of worn-out prison shoes. A diverse congregation of inmates gathered in anticipation. At the front, beneath an overhead light, stood Darren Lindsey—aka Bishop —a man once known for enforcing the streets' law, now draped in the humble attire of a preacher.

Bishop looked over the faces before him. His own eyes, however, held a new purpose. The air was thick with the weight of their collective sins as Bishop started his sermon.

"Brothers," he began, "we stand at the crossroads of our lives, each one of us burdened by the mistakes that brought us to this place. But let me tell you, redemption is not an illusion. It is a choice, a journey that begins within."

His hands, once accustomed to darker deeds, now gestured with a grace that seemed to defy the steel bars that enclosed them. "In the darkest corners of our souls, there exists a ray of light, a divine spark that yearns to illuminate our path. It's easy to believe that our sins define us, but it takes strength to realize that they do not condemn us."

Bishop's sermon wove through tales of biblical parables, drawing parallels to their struggles. The men, some skeptical at first, found themselves captivated by his words. His voice resonated, having walked in their shoes.

"We are not here to serve a life sentence in despair," he continued, his eyes locking onto each listener, "but to embrace the opportunity for salvation. Our past does not define us, brothers. It's what we choose to do today, in this very moment, that shapes our destiny."

As he spoke, the atmosphere shifted. The chapel transcended prison walls, lifting the weight of their sins. Bishop's sermon became a lifeline, offering hope in the confined darkness —a power that could emerge even in the most desolate of places.

Sentenced to 50 years, Bishop found a path unlike any other. He could have succumbed to the darkness that roamed the prison environment. However, something inside of him changed.

As the days turned into months, Bishop's transformation became clear. No longer a purveyor of the streets, he set his sights on a higher calling. The prison library became his sanctuary, where he devoured theological texts, his new passion for the divine eclipsing the memories of his criminal past.

A year into his sentence, Bishop's journey took an unexpected turn. The street-smart enforcer was transitioning into an ordained preacher. His fellow inmates, skeptical, witnessed a genuine metamorphosis that defied the hardened expectations of prison life.

In the confines of his cell, he forged an oath to himself— one that transcended the devil's work he had once embraced. Through the pages of the Bible, Bishop discovered a different strength—one that would guide him on the right track, even within the shadows of incarceration.

In her apartment, Justice packed away the remnants of a life she could no longer afford. The spacious loft, once a symbol of aspiration, was now filled with the emptiness of shattered dreams. As she sealed one of the last boxes, a worn photograph slipped into view—a captured moment of a happier time. It was her, her brother Jamal, and their dad.

Regret tugged at her gut as she traced the contours of their smiling faces frozen in the frame. Memories flooded her mind —of laughter, of simpler times, of a family that once stood together. Still, the reality of the present time crashed over her like a tsunami.

Grief hugged Justice as she struggled with the truth. Her father and mother were gone, and Jamal—once her responsibility—was imprisoned in the federal penitentiary and distant. The emotions became too much to bear, and Justice, overcome by the weight of her failures, crumbled.

In the quiet corner of her loft, she allowed herself to mourn the broken expectations, the choices that led her astray, and the family she couldn't salvage. Tears streamed down her face as she confronted her mistakes. She felt the pain of letting down the ones who believed in her—her father, her mother, and especially Jamal.

As Justice cried, she felt the release of emotion, an acknowledgment of the pain that clung to her past. The loft was now a witness to a life she had built and the irreversible fractures that scarred her soul.

Unlike most of Luck's crew, Justice slipped through the tight grip of the legal system. Her cooperation had played a significant role in dismantling one of New York City's most notorious criminal factions, sparing her from the confines of a jail cell. However, the absence of prison bars didn't equate to freedom; instead, it marked the beginning of a life lived in constant fear.

Potential threats tainted every passing second, and Justice found herself in a dance with paranoia. The dismantling of Luck's empire came at a cost—her peace of mind. Fearful and haunted, she couldn't escape the constant vigilance, always on the lookout for hidden dangers.

As she readied herself to depart the loft, the weight of her unfulfilled aspirations burdened her. Justice recognized the potential within herself, but the suffocating embrace of the streets had stifled her aspirations. This lifestyle captured dreams, drowned ambitions, and left only remnants.

Closing the door to the loft was a last gesture of leaving her past behind. With each step away, she expected a new chapter. Seeking change, Justice yearned for a life disconnected from enduring limitations. The unknown lay ahead, and a blank canvas awaited the strokes of redemption and reinvention.

The freezing winds sliced through the alleyway, carrying the stench of misery and lost dreams. Keisha huddled against the brick wall, her trembling hands squeezing a tattered jacket around her shivering frame. Once full of life, she now looked like she was on the verge of death.

The neon lights from the liquor store across the street cast shadows on Keisha's sunken face. Her eyes, once bright with confidence, now held the weight of guilt and regret. A lonely tear slipped down her cheek as memories of the courtroom replayed in her mind.

She reached into the pocket of her torn jeans, retrieving a small plastic baggie containing a temporary escape from reality. Beneath the light of a streetlamp, the contents glistened.

There was a momentary illusion of peace brought by the first hit. Her lips held a cold, metallic taste, serving as a bitter reminder of the depths to which she had fallen. As the drugs took effect, numbing her senses and drowning out the constant noise of her troubled thoughts, the alley became a blur.

Keisha reminisced about a time when laughter was pure and family held greater significance. A fading image of her innocent child's face sparked a pang of remorse. The courts had deemed her unfit, an unfit mother caught up in the clutches of her own demons.

Lost in the depths of the addiction, Keisha's journey through the streets had become a quest for oblivion. Her hair hung in disheveled strands, and the corners of her eyes held the wrinkles from sleepless nights haunted by the ghosts of her past.

A distant clock tower struck midnight, its chimes a sign of the time slipping away. Keisha's eyes reflected the fractured pieces of a soul damaged. The drugs offered a temporary escape, but the morning sun would bring with it the reality she sought to run away from.

She stood there, silent. She was a lost soul adrift in the unforgiving currents of life. The surrounding city, a metronome counting down the seconds until the next wave of torment crashed into her fragile existence.

The grand ballroom was bathed in dim lighting as they honored federal agents, Robert Parker and Samantha Mills, for their exceptional work in bringing down Luck and his crew. Their colleagues, superiors, and dignitaries gathered around for this special awards ceremony.

Agent Parker stepped up to the stage, the spotlight focusing on him as he stood tall behind the podium. The audience quieted, awaiting his words. With a deep breath, he began his speech.

"Thank you all for being here tonight," he started, eyes scanning the room. "This honor goes beyond a personal achievement. It's a culmination of a promise I made to myself and a legacy left by my father."

Silence fell over the room as everyone listened.

"I grew up watching my dad lace up his boots every morning, heading out to protect our community as a police officer," Parker continued. "He was my hero. But one day, he didn't come back. He gave his life in the line of duty, and from that moment, my path was clear."

He paused, the weight of his words hanging in the air.

"I became a federal agent not just to enforce the law, but to carry on my father's legacy. To make our streets safer for everyone. And tonight, as we celebrate a successful operation against crime, I can't help but think of him and the countless others who have made sacrifices."

The audience was captivated. A collective sense of respect filled the room.

"Every arrest, every criminal taken off the streets, is a step toward fulfilling that promise. We are the guardians of justice, and together, we stand against those who threaten the peace we hold dear."

The applause that followed shook the ballroom. Agent Parker nodded in gratitude, his eyes filled with the pride and responsibility he carried.

As the ceremony continued, the agents received their awards, marking a moment of triumph in their careers. Agent Parker and Agent Mills stood side by side, expressions of humility on their faces. The accolades were for the entire law enforcement community, not just them.

Amidst the celebration, Parker reflected on their journey here. He thought about the sleepless nights, the investigations, and the risks they took to dismantle Luck's criminal empire. It wasn't just a job; it was a mission rooted in a deep sense of duty.

As the night went on, Parker mingled with his colleagues, receiving congratulations, praise and sharing old stories. The atmosphere buzzed with accomplishment, a rare victory in the ongoing battle against crime.

By his side was Agent Mills. Her dedication to justice was clear in every move she made. United, they embodied the resilience of those who stood against criminality.

The ceremony signified both closure and new beginnings. With Luck and his crew behind bars, the city felt a little safer. Yet, both agents knew that the battle against crime persisted, an eternal tale of justice against peace disruptors.

As they left the ceremony, Parker looked over the city. Glittering lights below assure him that even in darkness, there are torchbearers of justice.

❧ 14 ❦

The day had arrived. After what felt like an eternity, the iron gates of the federal prison creaked open, granting Jamal an early release to his long-awaited freedom. As he stepped out into the open air, he took a deep breath, savoring the scent of his newfound liberty.

The world outside had changed since Jamal's incarceration, but the biggest transformation was within himself. Prison had chiseled away at his exterior, revealing a man who had weathered the storms of confinement and emerged with a new perspective on life.

The toll was clear. Jamal now walked with a slight limp due to being stabbed with a prison shank. Yet, despite the scars, his determination fueled him to continue on. The past was behind him, and he was ready to embrace the opportunities that lay ahead.

In the weeks leading up to his release, Jamal and Justice had rekindled their brother/sister connection. Their conversations bridged the gap that had widened during his time behind bars. Justice expected his return, having worked hard to preserve the barbershop that symbolized a fresh start for Jamal.

As the prison gates closed behind him, Jamal faced a world full of uncertainties and new possibilities.

The bell above the barbershop door chimed as Justice swept the floor. The constant noise from the clippers and the low buzz of conversations formed the familiar melody of the shop. As she worked, her mind raced with a whirlwind of emotions.

The door swung open, and a gust of wind carried in the city's sounds. Justice looked up, and there he was—Jamal, standing at the threshold.

Time slowed as their eyes locked. Outside vanished, leaving only the siblings locked in a silent embrace. Jamal's eyes traveled over the barbershop, taking in the familiar sights, but most importantly, the person he had missed the most.

Justice dropped the broom she was holding, and before she could process what was happening, she found herself wrapped in Jamal's arms. Their tight embrace sought to bridge years of separation with sheer closeness.

"Jamal," she whispered, her voice barely audible, choked up with emotion. She pulled back to look at him, her hands cupping his face as if reassuring herself that he was indeed real.

His eyes held a depth of experience. In that moment, the joy of reunion overshadowed past scars and hardships.

"I missed you, sis," Jamal told her.

Justice fought back tears, unable to articulate the flood of emotions that swirled inside of her.

The barbershop continued its steady cadence around them. The world outside was oblivious to the reunion taking place within its walls. Jamal's fingers traced the contours of the barbershop chair, memories flooding back, and Justice couldn't help but smile through the tears.

"You're home, Jamal," she said, her voice breaking through the emotional haze. The words carried a sense of relief, as if they had been waiting for this moment.

And in that barbershop, surrounded by conversations, laughter, and the rhythm of life, Justice and Jamal began the delicate process of rebuilding what time and circumstances had taken away—family, love, and the shared journey of redemption.

The barbershop buzzed with the lively chatter of clients sharing stories and laughter. Jamal, having honed his skills, was in his element, crafting haircuts that reflected both precision and artistry. His reputation as a master barber had spread, drawing clients from all over the city.

Justice, observing her brother's success, couldn't help but feel a sense of pride. The barbershop, once a symbol of turmoil, had transformed into a thriving business where people sought Jamal's expertise and camaraderie.

On a regular afternoon, the doorbell chimed, signaling the entrance of a new customer. Jamal turned around from his current client, catching sight of the stranger who stepped into the shop. The atmosphere shifted as their eyes met, curiosity lingering in the air.

"You Jamal?" the stranger inquired.

Jamal, accustomed to welcoming new clients, replied with a friendly nod. "Yeah, that's me."

"Can I get a haircut?" the stranger asked, taking a seat.

"Of course you're next. I'm just finishin' up here," Jamal assured, his professional demeanor masking any underlying tension. As he continued, the barbershop maintained its vibrant energy, unaware of the events that would soon unfold.

As Jamal worked on the new customer's haircut, his phone buzzed with alerts. He couldn't help but notice the persistent notifications from Justice. Glancing down at his phone, he saw her message inquiring about dinner plans.

Texting back a quick response, "Take out," Jamal refocused on the task at hand, ensuring that his client received the best haircut possible. Once satisfied with his work, he grabbed a small mirror from his workstation, offering the customer a chance to inspect the finished result.

"I like it," the man exclaimed, standing up from the barber's chair. He admired his reflection in the mirror, revealing a satisfied smile that showcased a row of pearly white teeth.

"How much do I owe you?" the man asked as he put on his jacket.

"Twenty-five," Jamal replied, his attention divided between the transaction and his buzzing phone—another message from Justice, but he ignored it for the moment.

Jamal's customer pulled a wad of cash from his pocket. Counting out fifty dollars, he handed the money to Jamal.

"I didn't get your name..." Jamal began, reaching out to accept the payment.

The man pulled him close, whispering, "Pedro," into his ear.

Simultaneously, he retrieved a knife from his back pocket and plunged it deep into Jamal's abdomen.

Jamal's eyes widened, and his breath quickened. Blood streamed from his mouth, down the side of his neck, as he collapsed to the floor with a thud. The few patrons inside the barbershop fled in panic.

Pedro stood over Jamal's body, bent down, and put his ear to Jamal's mouth to make sure he wasn't breathing. After a moment, he wiped the blood from his knife and his hand, adjusted his jacket, and exited the barbershop, leaving behind the aftermath of the bloody attack.

When Justice pulled up to the barbershop, the lingering crowd, police officers scattered throughout the area, and yellow tape blocking off the entrance shocked her. She grabbed the bag of takeout for herself and Jamal, then left her vehicle to investigate the commotion.

As she crossed the street, her eyes fell on a disheveled figure curled up beside the alleyway, about 1000 feet from the barbershop. The person looked up at Justice. Their eyes met. Justice swore she recognized this person, but she couldn't pinpoint it at the moment. The woman's face looked familiar.

"Karma done showed her face…" the woman mumbled, and Justice kept walking towards the barbershop. A few feet from the entrance, a patrol officer stopped her.

The officer held up his hand to halt Justice's progress. "Ma'am, you can't go any further. This is an active crime scene."

Justice, still shocked and confused, stammered, "What… wait… what happened? That's my brother's barbershop!"

The officer, recognizing Justice, lowered his hand and sighed. "I'm sorry, ma'am. There's been an incident. Your brother... he didn't make it."

Justice felt the ground shift underneath her feet. "What? No, no, that can't be... What happened?" Her voice trembled.

The officer hesitated, gauging how much to reveal. "There was an attack. He didn't survive. We're investigating, but it seems targeted."

As the weight of his words sank in, Justice felt a plethora of emotions—grief, anger, and an unsettling realization that the dangerous world they thought they left behind had now claimed her brother's life.

In the middle of the commotion, the disheveled woman from the alley approached, eyes red and weary. "Justice... you don't remember me?"

Justice squinted, trying to place the face. "I'm sorry, do I know you?"

The woman sighed. "It's Keisha... Luck's sister. We used to be friends."

Justice's eyes got big as she recognized her. "Keisha? What happened to you?"

Keisha's eyes dropped. "I lost everything. Just like you're losing now."

Questions flooded Justice's mind. *Who would target Jamal? Why now? And what connection did Keisha have to all of this?* The answers were elusive, buried beneath the layers of a complex and dangerous past.

Jamal's funeral was solemn, with few mourners present. Among the attendees, Justice was surprised to see his swimming coach from Lincoln High School in the midst of the subdued atmosphere. However, what rattled her even more was the unexpected presence of federal agents, Robert Parker and Samantha Mills, who waited until the ceremony concluded before approaching her.

As the last few moments of the service unfolded, Justice felt the weight on her shoulders. The reality of her brother's tragic death was settling in. Once the ceremony concluded, she stood by the graveside, staring at the casket being lowered into the ground. Soon, Jamal's headstone would be placed right next to their mother and fathers.

It was then that Agents Parker and Mills approached.

"Ms. Carter, we're sorry for your loss," Agent Mills began, her tone measured but genuine.

Justice nodded. "Thank you."

Agent Parker added, "We know this is a difficult time for you, but we wanted to talk to you about Jamal."

Justice's eyebrows went up. "What about him?"

Agent Mills hesitated. "We've been investigating certain activities, and Jamal might have become entangled in a dangerous situation. We need your cooperation to understand his connections and the events leading to his... tragic end."

"What are you talking about? Jamal was just a barber. He got caught up in something that wasn't his fault."

Agent Parker exchanged a glance with Mills before responding, "We believe there's more to it, Ms. Carter. And we believe you might have information that could help us untangle the truth."

"Untangle what truth? My brother is dead. What more do you want?"

The agents maintained their composed demeanor. "We're not here to accuse anyone, Ms. Carter. We want to understand what happened. You can help bring clarity to the situation."

Justice, caught between grief and the desire to know the full story behind Jamal's murder, took a deep breath. "Fine. Let's talk..."

A few days had passed since Jamal's death, and Justice mustered the courage to enter the shop again.

As she pushed open the door, the soft chime of bells overhead sounded her entrance. She couldn't help but recall the times her father had run the shop, putting smiles on every person's face who sat in his barber chair. But reality smacked her as she glanced down at the blood-stained floor. It was a reminder of Jamal's helplessness.

To regain control, Justice went to the backroom. Grabbing a wash rag and a bucket of water, she kneeled beside the blood stain. With each scrub, memories and tears intertwined, creating a poignant symphony of grief and resilience.

Justice lost herself in the repetitive motion, a silent catharsis as she tried to cleanse not only the physical mark but also the emotional scars left by the recent events. The intense scrubbing became a desperate attempt to erase the traces of tragedy.

Tears washed her face as she scrubbed, and scrubbed, the pain manifesting in each movement. Everybody was gone—her mother, her father, her brother, and the sense of security the barbershop once provided. The space had transformed into a sorrowful, haunted sanctuary.

Lost in her thoughts, the entrance of Keisha startled Justice. The bells at the front door jingled, pulling her from the trance. Keisha's presence, unexpected but somehow comforting, introduced a momentary pause in the struggle against the stain and the weight of her grief.

"He didn't deserve that…" Keisha's voice carried a heaviness, mirroring the weight of the washrag in Justice's hand. "Jamal was just a kid," Keisha continued. "A kid who knew nothing about what he was getting into. I give you my condolences, Justice, and I pray for you…"

Justice dropped the rag, releasing the burden she carried. She looked up into Keisha's eyes. Despite the trauma and hurt, Keisha extended genuine condolences and prayers, a small but meaningful gesture in the face of tragedy.

A half-smile played on Justice's lips. "Thank you, Keisha."

Keisha, sensing Justice's need for answers, gathered the strength to confess, "I know who did this."

Justice stood up. "You know who did what?" she questioned.

"I know who killed Jamal, Justice. It was Pedro Ramirez," Keisha admitted.

Justice remembered Luck mentioning the Ramirez cartel. They wanted retribution for what Jamal did to Pedro's nephew. The truth hit her like a wave. Tears welled up, and she cried until her eyes were dry.

"Look, I know you probably hate me right now," Keisha expressed. "And I don't blame you. But I can't shake this guilt, Justice. What happened to Jamal… it's eating me alive."

Justice studied Keisha's face, searching for sincerity. Keisha told the truth about her involvement in the trial, her regrets, and her genuine desire to help Justice find the answers she needed.

"Helping you won't bring Jamal back, but it's a start," Keisha said, her eyes pleading for understanding.

Bishop sat in his cramped quarters in the federal prison. He flipped through the newspaper, scanning the headlines that connected him to the world outside the prison walls. The monotonous routine of life behind bars had become his reality, and the newspaper provided a link to the events transpiring beyond the steel bars.

As his eyes moved across the pages, a shocking headline caught his attention: *"Barbershop Owner Slain in Brutal Attack."* He squinted at the accompanying photo, revealing Jamal's smiling face from happier times. Disbelief and sorrow washed over Bishop.

"Lord, have mercy," Bishop mumbled under his breath, his eyes closing as he clutched the paper in his hands. Thoughts of the young man flooded his mind, the boy who had sought guidance and mentorship. The news of Jamal's death was unexpected.

Bishop felt a burden on his soul as he considered the potential culprits. His thoughts gravitated toward Luck, the man whose influence reached beyond the prison walls. The realization brought a moment of silence before Bishop bowed his head in prayer.

"Lord, I lift up the soul of Jamal Carter before you. May he find peace in your eternal embrace. Grant strength to those who mourn his loss," Bishop prayed, the words spoken with a sincerity that resonated through the stillness of his confined quarters.

With the prayer said, Bishop folded the newspaper, tucking it under his arm. Conflicting emotions burned inside of him—grief for Jamal, anger at the injustice, and a tremendous sense of responsibility. The ordained preacher, once trapped in the web of criminality, contemplated the path ahead, knowing that his past continued to paint long shadows over his present.

Bishop was pondering his future when a Corrections Officer entered.

"Lindsey, you're on the pack-up," the officer stated.

"Excuse me?" Bishop responded in confusion.

"Looks like you're on a transfer," he explained.

"A transfer?" Bishop was confused. He had not requested a transfer. "You sure you got the right guy?" he questioned.

The officer glanced down at the paperwork, then handed it to Bishop.

"That's you, correct?"

Bishop looked at the document, confirming that it bore his name and information.

The officer sensed Bishop's reluctance and the uncertainty. "I'll give you a few minutes to get your things together, and I'll be back," he informed him.

Bishop sulked in his chair, angered with the unwelcoming news of a transfer. A move to a new facility was the last thing he needed. It would force him to start at the bottom again. The lack of information about his transfer destination added to Bishop's frustration, especially since dealing with the federal authorities was unpredictable and could result in being shipped across the country without warning.

Luck pulled himself up on the pull-up bar for the hundredth time until his chin was level with it, his muscles straining with each repetition. He then transitioned into 100 pushups, displaying a relentless determination. After completing the grueling exercise, he put his sweatshirt back on and took a seat at a nearby bench to catch his breath.

A few seconds later, a chubby man with waves and gold wire-framed glasses approached Luck. "You see this shit?" he said, handing over a newspaper. Luck glanced over the headline, and the moment he spotted Jamal's picture, he knew who was responsible for the murder. Shaking his head, he passed the newspaper back to the chubby man.

"That's fucked up. But, wassup wit' that other thing?" Luck inquired.

"It's in motion..." Chubby replied. "He should be pullin' up tonight."

A sinister smile played on Luck's lips as he acknowledged the update. The wheels of a plan, buried in secrecy and vengeance, were turning, and Luck was ready to see it unfold.

Navigating the federal prison yard is the first step for an inmate to establish their position within the prison hierarchy, where power, danger, and survival are displayed in a complex dance of dominance. In this arena, inmates scrutinize every step taken, and alliances are formed amidst an undercurrent of menace. This space is a melting pot of illicit activities, from the trade of drugs to extortion plots hatched in whispered conversations. Gang rivalries play out in the open, with tensions often escalating into brutal, bloody confrontations. Sexual assaults, a harrowing reality, puts fear in the hearts of the vulnerable. And murder, the ultimate manifestation of power, can linger in the air like an unspoken threat.

LATER THAT NIGHT

The prison yard was booming with activity despite the biting cold that gripped the air. Inmates went about their dealings, navigating drug trades, gang activity, and the typical hustle that defined prison life. Luck, flanked by two accomplices, watched from a vantage point near a weathered bench. Amidst the regular chaos, something drew his attention, and with a subtle nod, he signaled his accomplices to take notice. The chubby man with waves and gold-wire glasses, ever loyal to Luck's command, inquired about how to handle the situation.

Luck flashed his signature smile. "Make it ugly." He ordered and walked away from the bench, leaving his two accomplices to handle their business.

Bishop walked the expansive prison yard. The vast space, populated by inmates engaged in their nightly activities, felt like a world unto itself. The air was thick with tension, and Bishop observed the complex social dynamics at play. Inmates huddled in groups, their conversations veiled in secrecy, while others engaged in solitary contemplation, marking their territory in this volatile microcosm.

He carefully picked a neutral spot on an empty bench,

mindful of the territorial boundaries that governed the dynamics of the yard. With a conscious effort to keep a low profile, he pulled his wool hat down over his ears and retrieved a small Bible from inside his coat. As he opened the sacred book, his eyes landed on a passage that resonated with the surrounding atmosphere—a scripture that spoke of deception and the shadows that lurked in the human soul. In the glow of the prison yard lights, Bishop immersed himself in the words.

"The wisdom of the prudent is to understand his way, but the folly of fools is deceit."

As he absorbed the words in the passage, two men suddenly interrupted his contemplative moment. One of them was chubby with waves and gold-wire-framed glasses.

"Got a light, brother?" the chubby man asked, cigarette in hand.

Bishop rose to his feet. His attention on the chubby man as he replied, "I don't smoke."

Chubby smirked. "You must be the new guy," he said. The other man, a tall and wiry figure, remained silent but watched Bishop.

"Yeah, just got in," Bishop replied, tucking his Bible back into his coat pocket. The prison yard was notorious for testing newcomers, and Bishop was no exception.

"What they call you?" Chubby asked.

Unfazed by the casual exchange, he responded, "Bishop..." But, before the last syllable left his lips, his eyes shifted to the tall, wiry guy removing a makeshift prison shank from beneath his coat. The cold steel shined in the yard's light as the wiry guy lunged toward Bishop.

Bishop, anticipating trouble, sidestepped the attack, pulling his own makeshift prison shank. Although smaller, Bishop crafted it with deadly intent. Cocking his arm, he swung the shank with the precision of a professional baseball player, landing a targeted blow to the tall wiry guy's neck.

Blood soaked his sweatshirt, and the tall wiry guy collapsed to the ground. A gunshot sounded through the yard, prompting most inmates to hit the floor in a rapid response. But Bishop and Chubby remained standing, caught in a moment.

Chubby, sensing the need to finish the hit, retrieved his own weapon and charged at Bishop, delivering a strike to his face. Chubby gained the upper hand, positioning himself on top of Bishop. Another gunshot pierced the air, but Chubby paid it no mind, persisting in his assault. Stabbing at Bishop, he raised his arm for one last stab when a third shot rang out, causing Chubby to collapse beside his target.

Bishop, in excruciating pain, rolled onto his side, his hands clutching at his chest where blood was seeping through his fingers. With the little strength he had, he reached into his coat pocket and pulled out the blood-stained bible. The holy book had a hole through its middle, and Bishop realized it had acted as a shield, blocking the deadliest strike that was aimed at his heart. Gripping the book in his bloody hands, he held onto it until the COs rushed in, clearing the yard of inmates.

Luck found himself on the cold concrete, the side of his face pressed into the gravel, hands secured behind his back. He had observed the chaotic scene unfold from a distance, and when the first warning shot pierced the air, he took cover.

As the correctional officers pulled him off the ground, his eyes surveyed the aftermath. Chubby lay sprawled in a pool of his own blood, his gold-wire-framed glasses laying inches away from his stiff body, and his accomplice shared a similar fate on the pavement. Glancing around, Luck's eyes settled on Bishop being helped to his feet by the COs. Bishop was still breathing, still alive, still walking. Shaking his head, Luck couldn't help but acknowledge the folly of sending amateurs to do a man's job.

❧ 15 ❧

The dark parking deck thumped with the bass from the underground nightclub. General Lee, dressed in his usual Champion hoodie, army fatigue and Timberland boots, leaned against his Range Rover, the smoke from his cigar swirling into the night air. Becoming more impatient, he crushed the cigar against the back tire as the headlights of a Maserati pierced the shadows.

The luxury car rolled to a stop, and Lee straightened up. Behind his dark shades, he fixed his eyes on the driver. The door swung open, revealing a dressed figure stepping out. The smell of danger lingered as Lee approached.

"You been dodging my calls, Tommy. Dodging your responsibilities."

"I had some setbacks, Lee. You know how it is."

General Lee's eyes narrowed. His patience was wearing thin. "Setbacks don't erase debts. You owe me, and you know the consequences of not paying up."

Tommy whispered. "Look, Lee, I've got something big in the works. Once it goes through, I'll settle up with you. I promise."

"Something in the works? I heard that shit before. I need my twenty-five percent, Tommy."

Making sure his appearance was in order, Tommy smoothed his slacks and secured his gun on his waist. "General, you're asking for a piece that's too big. You're here because you know my operation is vast."

"I don't give a fuck about your operation, Tommy. You play in my city, that means you pay the toll. Simple as that."

Tommy glanced over his shoulder as if he was expecting trouble. He reached into his suit jacket and produced a stack of cash. "Here, take it," he said, gritting his teeth. "But this is the last time you squeeze me like this."

Lee smiled as he counted the stack of bills.

"I heard something you might find interesting." Tommy said, switching the subject.

"Oh, yeah... what's that?"

"Justice... she's back. Back around the old barbershop."

Lee stopped in mid-count and looked Tommy in his eyes. "Justice, huh?"

Tommy nodded, beads of sweat forming on his forehead. "Yeah, I saw her myself. You know how she is... trouble."

Lee smirked. "Well, well, well... Seems like our lil' rendezvous might have to wait, Tommy. I got some unfinished business to tend to."

The men went separate ways, each with their own agenda.

General Lee, consumed by money and recent revelations, failed to notice Tommy's double-crossing. After facing an out-of-state drug trafficking charge, Tommy had struck a deal with the feds to maintain his freedom.

In the streets of Corona, Queens, Tommy Brown had a reputation as a drug trafficker. Once a kingpin of his domain, Tommy's reign faced an abrupt challenge with the emergence of General Lee, a former soldier whose demeanor eclipsed even the seasoned gangster's reputation.

A true thug at heart, Tommy exuded the charisma and cunning that defined his criminal enterprise. But, General Lee proved to be a more savage breed of gangster.

Caught in the crosshairs of Lee's pressure and intimidation, Tommy's empire crumbled. And after facing the heat from a trafficking charge that threatened to incinerate everything he had built, Tommy made a calculated decision—to turn the tables on the man who sought to crush him. He entered the world of cooperation with federal authorities. To survive the deadly game they were entwined in, he relied on outsmarting General Lee, resting his hopes on wits over brute force.

The question lingered: *Would his intellect be enough to outmaneuver General Lee, or was he destined to become another casualty in the streets of New York?*

In a nearby unmarked van, Agent Parker and Agent Mills exchanged glances as they monitored every word that Tommy and Lee said through hidden microphones.

TWO DAYS LATER

"I think that van is back..." Keisha said as she stepped inside the barbershop.

Justice, absorbed in her thoughts, looked up from the countertop cluttered with hair care products. "It's those agents again... they won't let up."

Wearied by the weight of recent events, Justice exhaled. The past months were a wild ride, with constant fear of more danger. The memory of her brother's murder served as a haunting backdrop, shaping the contours of her present reality.

In this storm of uncertainty, an unexpected bond had formed between Justice and Keisha. As Justice helped Keisha rebuild her life from the ruins of addiction, Keisha, in turn, became the support system that Justice needed. Their friendship, once fractured, was mending.

The barbershop, once a place for haircuts and camaraderie, now faced an uncertain future. Justice thought about shutting it down, a decision she made out of fear and the persistent threat hanging over them. The memories of cartel violence and the presence of federal agents had taken a toll on Justice's peace of mind. But during this turmoil, Keisha had a unique plan.

In a decision that symbolized a step toward a new beginning, Keisha proposed an idea. Instead of running away, they could renovate the space into a beauty salon and supply store. Justice, after contemplation, recognized the merit in Keisha's suggestion. The makeover not only embraced change, but also held the promise of a fresh start.

As the shop underwent its metamorphosis, Keisha took on the role of manager. The once-male-dominated environment now radiated with a feminine touch, embodying resilience and adaptability. Under Keisha's leadership, they strived to create a haven where healing and transformation could unfold, going beyond hair and beauty.

"Ever thought about their offer?" Keisha asked, her eyes shifting to the unmarked van outside.

Justice, focused on the vehicle, responded, "No. I'm done with them. All they've done is make my life a living hell."

Keisha nodded, "Couldn't agree more. And, really, they're wasting their time trying to get Luck to cooperate. It's just not happening."

Much needed laughter filled the air. The shared understanding between Justice and Keisha was clear. They both knew Luck's stubbornness—no force, be it coercion or threat, would make him budge.

"How's the process going trying to get Kiani back?" Justice inquired.

Keisha stopped what she was doing and thought about her daughter. It had been more than a year since she'd seen her, and she couldn't hold back the tears. "I'm trying, Justice..." she cried. "I'm doing all they told me to do, but it's not happening fast enough. I miss my baby..."

Justice, moved by Keisha's pain, stepped closer and offered a comforting embrace. "I can't imagine how tough this is for you. But you're doing everything you can, and I believe things will work out. Kiani needs her mom, and you're making the changes to be there for her."

Keisha nodded. "I just hope the courts see that I'm serious about turning my life around. I want to be the mother Kiani deserves."

Justice squeezed her hand. "You're on the right path, Keisha. Stay strong, and we'll get through this together."

The melodic chime of the bell danced through the air, announcing an unexpected visitor at the entrance of the salon. Justice, engrossed in a rare moment with Keisha, felt an unsettling jolt in her stomach muscles, a visceral premonition that trouble had arrived. As the door swung open, a subtle tension filled the room, and Justice's eyes locked onto the person stepping inside.

Keisha, attuned to the sudden shift in energy, pivoted on her heels, her strides carrying her toward the back room. She disappeared behind the door, leaving Justice alone to confront the stranger in the salon's entrance.

"I like what you've done with the place," General Lee remarked, his eyes scanning the transformed surroundings. A sly grin played on his lips as he continued, "Yeah, this could work..." He said, as he rubbed his hands together.

Outside, across the street, federal agents Wells and Parker sat in the unmarked van. Wells, focused on the unfolding scene, tapped her partner. "You see that, Parker?" Her eyes were on General Lee as he entered the salon.

Parker, finishing his sandwich, mumbled with a mouth full of food, "Yeah, I see..."

Wells leaned back in the driver's seat, contemplating their next move. "Give it a few minutes, and we'll go check it out," she instructed. They were determined not to miss the opportunity to catch General Lee in the act. So, with patience as their ally, they waited.

"Can I help you?" Justice asked, her eyes on Lee. She was well aware of who he was, but uncertain about his presence.

"You know who I am, right?" Lee questioned, looking for recognition in her eyes. Justice maintained her stare. "Okay, so, check this out," Lee continued, leaning in. "I'ma set something up in the back, run the customers through here, and we gon' make this a goldmine." He nodded. "This a nice muhfuckin' spot we got here..."

Justice's eyes narrowed as General Lee strolled further into the salon. He looked over the transformed space. The smell of freshly painted walls and hair products lingered in the air.

The overhead lights put a grim illumination on General Lee, revealing the lines in his face from years of ruthless dealings. His grin, more predatory than approving.

As Justice faced him, the room seemed to get smaller, amplifying the gravity of the moment. The floor creaked under Lee's weight, the sound punctuating the silence between them. The hum of the air conditioner competed with the rapid beat of Justice's heart.

A bead of sweat traced a path down the side of her face, evidence of the internal struggle between fear and resilience. The soft rustle of her clothing underscored the tension in her stance.

General Lee ran his fingers over the installed countertop, a sly smile playing on his lips. His movements were deliberate, each gesture a calculated step.

The distant wail of a police siren broke the room's silence.

Justice spoke. "Excuse me... we? Who the fuck are you?"

"How soon we forget..." he sneered.

With an almost theatrical swiftness, General Lee's hand went to his waist, fingers gripped around his forty caliber handgun. In one seamless motion, he brandished the weapon, the cold steel pressing against Justice's forehead.

In the back room, Keisha fumbled with the small, silver key. It had slipped from her grasp twice before she secured it.

Summoning a deep breath, she steadied her trembling hands and approached the safe in the corner. The glow from the digital keypad lit up her face as she punched in the code. A soft beep signaled the acceptance of the correct combination, and the heavy door of the three-foot safe was released with a muted click.

Keisha scanned the contents until her eyes locked onto the sleek silhouette of a nine-millimeter handgun. The cold metal gleaming under the light.

Time was a luxury they couldn't afford, and Keisha wasted none. She snatched the weapon from its resting place, the weight of it familiar and reassuring in her grip. Holding the cold steel in her hand brought back memories of the world they wanted to forget.

Without a second thought, Keisha darted back into the main area of the salon.

The loud sounds of gunshots disturbed the quietness outside the salon. Agents Wells and Parker, surprised, got low in the confines of the unmarked van, their hands reaching for the holsters securing their service weapons.

The agents exchanged an apprehensive glance.

The shots had come from the same place they'd been surveillancing

With silent communication born of shared experience, Wells and Parker coordinated their movements. They exited the van with cautious but purposeful steps, their eyes scanning the surroundings for any signs of danger.

Crossing the street with trained precision, the agents approached the entrance of the shop, their senses heightened and nerves on edge.

As Agent Parker pushed the door open, the pungent scent of gun-smoke invaded his nostrils. General Lee squirmed on the floor, clinging to life in a puddle of blood. Lee's eyes locked onto Parker's before he took his last breath and his body went limp.

Upon entering the shop, the agents encountered a gruesome sight. Justice lay sprawled in the middle of the floor, a stream of blood seeping from her head.

With their breath caught in their throats, the agents continued to move forward, their eyes drawn to the back of the shop. There, they saw Keisha, lying in a pool of blood, and right beside her, a pistol.

EPILOGUE
ONE YEAR LATER

In the chapel of the federal prison, Bishop stood at the makeshift pulpit. His eyes, once gleaming with street intensity, now reflected wisdom from life's trials. The congregation, a gathering of inmates, listened as Bishop began his sermon.

"Brothers and sisters, it's been a year—a year of reflection, growth, and redemption. In this place of confinement, where the steel bars surround us, it's easy to reminisce about the streets that once held us captive. But let me tell you something: the true captivity was not in the alleys or the corners where we hustled; it was in the mindset that led us there."

Bishop's voice resonated through the chapel, carrying the weight of experience. He continued, "I used to dream of luxury cars, designer clothes, and piles of money. I chased after those dreams with a fervor that blinded me to the reality of the choices I was making. The streets whispered promises of glory, but in reality, they paved the way for heartache, loss, and the deafening sound of sirens and gunshots."

The congregation leaned in, captivated by Bishop's words.

"Look at me now," Bishop declared, gesturing to the drab surroundings of the prison chapel. "The trappings of the street life led me to this very place, confined within these walls. But let me tell you, my confinement is not a punishment; it's an opportunity for rebirth, a chance to break free from the chains that bound my spirit."

He paced the small stage, his eyes scanning the faces of those before him. "I've seen the allure of the streets, the glittering facade that hides the reality. We were enticed by the promise of wealth, power, and respect, but what we got was pain, betrayal, and a one-way ticket to places like this."

Bishop's voice grew more impassioned. "Our young ones, our brothers and sisters out there, listen. These streets ain't for everybody. They don't love you; they'll chew you up and spit you out. The blocks and street corners of our neighborhoods that we claimed as territory were nothing more than illusions of control. In reality, we were controlled by the very streets we thought we owned."

He paused, letting the weight of his words settle. The silence in the chapel spoke volumes.

"But there is hope, my people. Redemption is not an abstract concept; it's a tangible reality waiting for those who are willing to reach for it. We must break the cycle, not just for ourselves, but for the generations that follow. It starts with understanding that true power lies not in the barrel of a gun or the stack of cash in your hand, but in the choices you make every day."

Bishop's eyes shifted to the high, barred windows, as if

seeking inspiration beyond the prison walls. "I've seen the worst of humanity, and I've been a part of it. But in the darkness, I found a light—a light that led me to redemption. It's never too late to change, to transform, to rise above the circumstances that once held us captive."

The congregation listened in rapt attention, their faces reflecting remorse, contemplation, and hope.

Bishop's voice lowered. "We must be architects of our own destinies, no longer swayed by the false promises of the streets. I implore you, my brothers and sisters, to use this time of confinement not as a sentence but as a sabbatical for the soul. Reflect on the paths that led you here, confront the demons within, and emerge stronger, wiser, and ready to rebuild."

He turned to the scripture, his tone shifting to one of spiritual guidance. "In the book of life, every chapter matters. Our past does not define us, but it shapes us. Seek forgiveness, not only from a higher power, but from within. Let the redemption you find in your heart be a beacon for others."

As Bishop concluded his sermon, the chapel echoed with a heartfelt amen from the congregation. Lives, once entangled, now found hope in new possibilities.

Bishop stood there as a testament to transformation, his words lingering in the air like a promise—a promise that, even in the darkest corners, redemption was within reach.

THE NEXT MORNING

Bishop adjusted his tie in the small mirror hanging on the wall of his cell. His reflection staring back at him. As he buttoned up his shirt, he recited a silent prayer for strength and guidance.

The prison tier was loud with the clinking of metal doors

and the distant sounds of inmates beginning their day. Bishop made his way through the narrow passageway, a sense of determination propelling each step. His role in reception and transfer was not just a way to fill the time.

As he entered the work area, he greeted his colleagues—fellow inmates who, like him, yearned for some normalcy within the confines of the prison walls. The reception desk, filled with paperwork and a fluorescent light, became his domain during the work hours.

Throughout the day, Bishop managed the transfer paperwork, ensuring that the administrative processes ran. His interactions with other inmates and the prison staff carried an air of calm and wisdom. Some sought his guidance, while others felt comfortable in the presence of someone who had walked a path similar to their own.

While fingering through some paperwork for incoming transfers, Bishop's eyes fell on a recognizable name. He couldn't believe what he was seeing. He blinked and adjusted his glasses, only to see the same name as before.

His fingers tightened around the paperwork as the name "Lucian Beckford" jumped off the page and into his consciousness. Memories flooded back with that name of darkness and violence surrounding him.

He adjusted his glasses again, hoping that the letters on the paper would rearrange themselves, that this revelation would prove to be a figment of his imagination. But it wasn't.

The hairs on his arms stood at attention, an involuntary response to the sinister chill that slithered through his body. Lucian Beckford—the very mention of that name reopened wounds that time had not healed. Bishop, a man of God, wrestled with the rage inside of him. The teachings of the Bible replaying in his mind, urging him to turn the other cheek, to forgive. But this was different. This was personal. His blood had been spilled, his life threatened, and almost taken. The scars on his body were receipts from the brutality he had endured.

Revenge, a word that clashed with the tenets of his faith, now lingered in the air like an uninvited guest. Bishop knew he had to act fast. The prison walls seemed to close in on him as he contemplated the choices ahead. In that moment, the man of God found himself at a crossroads, torn between the pulpit and the darkness that promised to conquer him once more.

The metal clinking sounded through the tier as the heavy doors opened, signaling the onset of the chow. Hundreds of inmates shuffled down the narrow steps, forming a disorganized procession en route to the mess hall. Amid the crowd, Lucian "Luck" Bedford moved with an air of authority, his demeanor reflecting the confidence of a seasoned boss.

Transferred overnight, Luck navigated the prison hierarchy solo. The absence of a crew didn't deter him; it only fueled him. Luck, a born soldier, had weathered storms on the streets, and the penitentiary was just another battlefield.

The prison walls, filled with an undercurrent of tension, seemed to part for Luck as he walked through the crowd. Eyes followed his every move, assessing the newcomer in their midst.

This prison might have been unfamiliar territory, but Luck's spirit remained unbroken. It didn't matter where he was, he was always a gangster.

Bishop stood at the entrance of the mess hall, his eyes studying the crowd of inmates. Patience was his ally as he waited for the right moment. During the chaotic shuffle, his eyes locked onto his target, a figure moving through the crowd.

With a calm and deliberate motion, Bishop eased a shank from its concealed position at his waistline. As the seconds ticked away, he prepared for the confrontation that was about to unfold, his focus on the man who had once threatened his life.

Luck's attention shifted as an approaching inmate greeted him. "Whaddup, my nigga?" the man exclaimed, extending his hand for a handshake. Luck studied the face before him. A sense of recognition flashed but didn't materialize. "Strike. You don't remember me?" the man continued, attempting to jog Luck's memory.

The name struck a chord, triggering a momentary lapse in Luck's attention. Before he could respond, Bishop emerged from the shadows, a homemade shank gripped tight in his hand. The energy shifted as Bishop's eyes locked onto Luck's. In that moment, Luck understood that the past had caught up with him, and he found himself tangled in the web of retribution.

The makeshift blade sank deep into Luck's abdomen, prompting an involuntary gasp of pain. His eyes widened in shock.

Bishop recited a prayer—an eerie, melodic cadence. "May the Lord have mercy on your soul, for the darkness within has consumed the light," he said.

As he continued the prayer, he stared into Luck's eyes. It was a silent communion, a soul-stirring connection that transcended the physical act of violence. The messhall seemed to hush in deference to this deadly moment between predator and prey.

The hospital air clung to Justice as she emerged from the unconsciousness, her eyes adjusting to the light filtering through the sheer curtains. A year in a coma brought physical and emotional challenges, but now, as she sat up in bed, her path to healing transformed.

Justice, once defined by the streets, stood at a new chapter's threshold.

As her bare feet made contact with the cool linoleum floor, a wave of vulnerability washed over her. The familiar antiseptic scent and medical equipment noise reminded her of her time on life's edge and the unknown.

Dressed in a simple hospital gown, Justice moved, her hand brushing against the IV stand as she made her way toward the window. The cityscape unfolded beyond the glass. Her reflection in the window revealed a woman reshaped by adversity—a survivor who had weathered the storms that raged within and around her.

In the solitude of the hospital room, Justice contemplated the lessons she had learned. The streets had led her down a path of destruction. Despite scars, she danced with shadows, confronted demons, and emerged unbroken.

THE END

AFTERWORD

A WARNING FROM THE STREETS: CHOOSE YOUR PATH WISELY

When considering Justice and Jamal's journey, it acts as a reminder to young individuals during a pivotal time in their lives. The streets may seem glamorous, filled with illusions of wealth, power, and respect. But beneath the surface lies a treacherous path, a path that often leads to destruction and heartache.

Social media, a double-edged sword in the digital age, can weave intricate tales of success and grandeur. It presents a facade, a curated narrative that can mislead the vulnerable into chasing shadows. The flashing lights and endless likes may seem fulfilling, but they pale in comparison to the genuine connections and accomplishments born from hard work, dedication, and education.

The streets may entice with promises of a quick route to validation, but the truth lies in the untold stories of broken families, shattered friendships, and the lives cut short. It's a long road to nowhere, a journey that leaves regret in its wake.

To the youth, I urge you: be cautious architects of your destiny. Do not succumb to the pressure of the moments that promise temporary gratification. There is no shame in being who you are, embracing your uniqueness, and walking the path less traveled—a path that leads to knowledge, growth, and self-discovery.

The streets, with their magnetic pull, may attempt to redefine your worth, but know this: your value transcends the superficial metrics of the hood. Be smart, go to school, and invest in yourself. The power to shape your future lies within the pages of books, the walls of classrooms, and the resilience of your spirit.

In life, focus on those who care for you, those who nurture your potential and celebrate your victories, big or small. Impress those who matter, not the transient faces passing through the stages of your journey.

As we close this chapter, let Jamal's story be a reminder that the streets may promise riches, but true wealth lies in the currency of knowledge, integrity, and genuine connections. Choose your path wisely, for the streets, though alluring, may lead you astray from the brilliance you were meant to become.